Walking with Bray toward the pier made her feel as if she was about to go before a firing squad.

She was too tired to come up with some story to appease him. If he asked for the truth, she had nothing else left to give him.

Why did she care so much what he thought of her? Because she didn't want him to run away. She needed an ally. She needed Bray.

As if he'd read her mind, he put his arm around her. She tried not to tremble, but life as she'd created it for them was about to fall apart. She wished with all her heart there was some way to put off the inevitable.

Her wish was granted as the earth began to rumble under her feet and an earsplitting explosion blew her world to bits.

PATRICIA ROSEMOOR

TRIGGERED RESPONSE

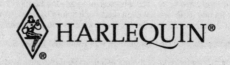

HARLEQUIN®

TORONTO • NEW YORK • LONDON
AMSTERDAM • PARIS • SYDNEY • HAMBURG
STOCKHOLM • ATHENS • TOKYO • MILAN • MADRID
PRAGUE • WARSAW • BUDAPEST • AUCKLAND

Triggered Response proved to be the most challenging book I've ever written.
It followed a year of tragedy—I lost four people dear to me in less than a year.
I dedicate this book to them.

In loving memory of my husband,
Edward Majeski, November 7, 1937–October 18, 2005,
and of my father, Walter Pinianski, October 17, 1917–February 10, 2005.
Also in loving memory of my aunt Jeannette Voelker, d. October 31, 2004,
and of my uncle Ray Fucci, d. August 2005.

I want to thank everyone who helped keep me sane and got me through 2005.
Linda Sweeney, Ruth Glick, Ann Voss Peterson, Sherrill Bodine,
Cheryl Jefferson, Rosemary Paulas, Jude Mandell, Cathy Andorka,
Arlene Erlbach, Elaine Sima, Judy Veramendi, Michael A. Black,
Julie Barrett, Denise Zaza, Tashya Wilson, Birgit Davis-Todd,
Jennifer Jackson, Marc Paoletti, Marcus Sakey,
Rob and Beth Flumignan, Julia Borcherts, Frank Crist,
Dana Litoff, Darwyn Jones, Megan Campbell,
Andre Frieden, Sharon Doering, Tina Hickman,
Florence Majeski, Scott and Alan Majeski; and numerous
other people for big and small kindnesses that kept me going.

ISBN-13: 978-0-373-22958-1
ISBN-10:   0-373-22958-5

TRIGGERED RESPONSE

Copyright © 2006 by Patricia Pinianski

www.eHarlequin.com

Printed in U.S.A.

ABOUT THE AUTHOR

Patricia Rosemoor has always had a fascination with dangerous love. In addition to her more than forty books for Harlequin Intrigue, she also writes for Harlequin Blaze and Silhouette Bombshell, bringing a different mix of thrills and chills and romance to each line.

She's won a Golden Heart Award from Romance Writers of America and Reviewers Choice and Career Achievement awards from *Romantic Times BOOKreviews*. She teaches writing popular fiction and suspense-thriller writing in the Fiction Writing Department of Columbia College Chicago. Check out her Web site: www.PatriciaRosemoor.com. You can contact Patricia either via e-mail at Patricia@PatriciaRosemoor.com, or through the publisher at Patricia Rosemoor, c/o Harlequin Books, 233 Broadway, Suite 1001, New York, NY 10279.

Books by Patricia Rosemoor

HARLEQUIN INTRIGUE

665—COWBOY PROTECTOR*
684—GYPSY MAGIC
       "Andrei"
703—FAKE I.D. WIFE**
707—VIP PROTECTOR**
745—BOYS IN BLUE
       "Zachary"
785—VELVET ROPES**
791—ON THE LIST**
858—GHOST HORSE
881—RED CARPET
       CHRISTMAS**
924—SLATER HOUSE
958—TRIGGERED RESPONSE

*The McKenna Legacy
**Club Undercover

CAST OF CHARACTERS

Brayden "Bray" Sloane—The security chief disappeared after a chemical explosion and hasn't been seen since. Does his vanishing act mean he's in trouble? Or is he to blame?

Claire Fanshaw—The computer expert is so desperate to find her friend that she convinces Bray Sloane that they're married, hoping that he'll remember something to help her.

Mac Ellroy—Did the lab tech orchestrate his own disappearance or did someone else, who wanted to keep him quiet?

Dr. Martin Kelso—The acting director of Cranesbrook Associates, Kelso is well connected, but with good or with evil?

Dr. Nelson Ulrich—The research director cares only about his work. To what lengths is he willing to go to protect it?

Hank Riddell—The research fellow seems to have all the answers and be in all the wrong places at all the right times.

Prologue

Three weeks before the accident

The light in the lab's storeroom was on.

Mac Ellroy was inside, checking the vials. Why the hell was the lab tech in here after hours? And what did he think he was doing messing with the chemicals?

"Find what you're looking for?"

Mac spun around, guilt all over his pretty face. His spiked hair seemed to stand on end as he choked, "I— I was just checking on things."

"Doing inventory?"

"R-right."

Mac was obviously lying. He was pretty much an open book. Not an ounce of subterfuge in him. None that was convincing, anyway.

"So where's your list?"

The lab tech looked around as if he really had one. "I, um, must have put it down somewhere.... Maybe it's out here."

Mac left the storeroom for the lab proper. One of the monkeys started chattering and a couple of the control rats skittered around their cages. Seeming oblivious to the familiar noises, Mac went from table to table as if he really might have put something down on one of them.

"Or maybe you're just snooping. Do you have a problem with your work?"

Mac stopped in front of the window. On the other side of the glass, moonlight shone down on the peaceful lake surrounded by small boulders and natural grasses. Framed as he was, not moving, not saying anything, the lab assistant looked like part of a still-life painting.

Then his square jaw tightened and the fine skin around his dark eyes pulled in little lines. "Don't you have a problem with it? Doesn't developing Project Cypress bother you? How do you sleep at night?"

"It's necessary work. We live in an unstable world."

"But this—"

"Is simply another tool to accomplish what's necessary. Obviously you don't agree."

"No, I don't."

"You'd be more comfortable being taken off this particular experiment, then."

Mac nodded. "I would rather work on something else."

"That can be arranged."

"Really? Good. Good." Mac breathed a sigh of relief. "But first you need to know that some of the chemicals are missing."

"Missing?" So he really had been taking inventory?

"I noticed one of the vials seemed a bit short. That's why I came back to the lab, to check the rest. Someone has tampered with the chemicals. You have a problem here."

"I know I do." He realized what he had to do wasn't pretty. "Why don't you show me?"

Eager now to share his findings, Mac turned toward the storeroom to lead the way. His mistake.

The fire extinguisher was on the wall, right there, right outside the storeroom door.

Mac never saw it coming.

Chapter One

Twelve days after the accident

His brain was on fire again.

He did his damnedest to stop from being sent to his private hell, but as always he was dragged kicking and screaming back into the raging inferno.

THE CRAGS OF HADES surround him, blazing hotter than the sun gone nova. The desert air is so intense that it blisters his skin. His mouth so dry that he can't swallow. Can hardly breathe.

He glances through dark glasses at the two men behind him. Both look like him—camouflage pants and armless T-shirts, heavy boots and helmets, carrying holstered pistols and K-bar knives and submachine guns. The mission went off as planned. They found the camp in the maze of caves and will use the GPS system to guide in the Afghani guerillas who'll route the enemy from their cover.

And then the American helicopters will take over.

Still, he has to be vigilant. The enemy could be

anywhere...waiting.... He senses danger like bugs crawling over him. One misstep and they're dead men.

Circling, he moves back against rock until their carefully sheltered Humvee comes into sight. Peering around between them and the vehicle, he sees no indication that the enemy is anywhere within shooting distance. Al Qaeda snipers could be positioned anywhere up in those rocks above them.

Sweat trickles down his spine as he signals the other men. Though they're all equipped with radios and headsets, he figures better to keep from making a sound. He indicates they should get back to the truck. He'll cover them and bring up the rear.

He raises his MP-5, ready to trigger the submachine gun at the slightest movement, at the smallest hint of light reflected off an enemy's weapon.

The seasoned guy goes first.

Trigger-finger tense, he turns this way and that, vigilant as his buddy goes for the driver's door. He signals the other one, the youngest kid in their unit. His dark skin is ashen, but if he's afraid, that's the only sign.

Running for the vehicle, the kid takes a fatal step, explodes like a child's piñata. Instead of candy and toys, his body bursts into bits of flesh and bone.

And blood. Pink mist.

Covered with the kid's life force, he loses it and runs to the Humvee. His gorge in his throat, he throws himself into the passenger seat, his driver buddy's tortured-sounding curses ringing in his ears. The vehicle takes off, throwing him hard back against the seat.

Something inside him finally breaks. An inner explo-

sion inside his head. He can't breathe. Even closing his eyes can't erase the image of another senseless death heaped on dozens of others he's seen.

His brain is on fire.

Burning. Melting.

But he has to be okay. Has to. People are counting on him. His Special Ops unit…the ones who aren't dead yet. The government that sent him here. The people back home.

He has to be okay. Has to.

He forces back the flames.

Only to have a second flash of sound open his eyes.

An explosion throws a wall of heat at him. Amid rubble and smoke, a white lab-coated body lies there at his feet. Not the kid. Not in the mountainous desert. Not all those years ago. Somehow he traverses through space and time. A different place, a different explosion, a different victim…

"No! Not again!"

Flying up out of the nightmare, he realized he'd been asleep in the bunk in the Baltimore homeless shelter where he'd been placed. He began to shake. His brain was on fire. Burning again as it had night after night after night. He fought back and pushed the images away as he always did because he had to be okay. *Had to.*

Whoever he was.

SECURITY EXPERT SOUGHT For Questioning.

The headline glared up at Claire Fanshaw as she picked up the *Baltimore Sun* on the way to her office on the opposite corridor from the Cranesbrook Asso-

sponsible and bring them and their damn project to their knees?

Thinking that far ahead scared Claire. Even though she didn't always tell the truth, she was basically a good person with an ability that gave her more power than sometimes made her comfortable. She was only doing this because something had happened to her best friend, Mac Ellroy.

Taking a deep breath, she decided to make another attempt to crack the password.

She brought up the program and clicked on Start. Numbers flashed across the screen as the multiplier compiled one hundred possible ways in to Project Cypress. It would take her at least an hour to go through these potential passwords. She cut and pasted the first number into her encryption program.

If only she could get to those computer files that might provide some explanations, then maybe she could settle down, get rid of the paranoia that followed her around like a black cloud.

The first number she tried didn't work—no big surprise, she'd been doing this for weeks now—so she cut and pasted the next in line.

The work on Project Cypress had triggered an explosion in the lab itself and far-reaching chaos within the company. Now, less than two weeks later, several people were dead—Cranesbrook's CEO, one of the security guards and two cops. Who knew if Wes Vanderhoven would ever be himself again, his mind having been affected by the accident.

The second try gave her another error message.

In some kind of bizarre coincidence, Zoe Sloane

had been kidnapped. How in the world did a baby fit into the picture other than through her relationship to her uncle, the missing security chief?

She entered number three.

A knock at her office door jarred Claire back to her job. "Come in," she said, even as she tapped a key that set her screen saver to life.

Her heart nearly stopped when Dr. Ulrich entered. The fiftyish scientist wore his lab coat buttoned one off and his graying blond hair styled in a comb-over that didn't fool anyone into believing he wasn't going bald.

He peered at her through wire-rimmed glasses, saying, "I need some information about a new computer program that will help us organize the results of our research. Can you have someone get that for me?"

"Of course, I'll do it myself." She picked up a pen and held it poised over a pad of paper. "The name of the program?"

"Bio-Chem Tracker."

"Got it."

Ulrich stood there, staring down at her as though he expected her to get him the information right this moment. Her pulse skittered through her veins. Her computer was still working on the password to his project, and if she took off the screen saver, he would see the big error message that was bound to be there and know what she was up to.

"Is there something more you need?" she asked, keeping her voice pleasant. "Information on another program?"

"Don't you just…pull it off your computer?" He waved his hand in the air as if he were trying to pull a rabbit from a hat.

"Oh, you want it now." She gave him an expression that was at once distressed and conciliatory. "I have some work that I need to get to for Dr. Kelso first, you understand. Unless this takes priority, of course."

"Everything in its order, I suppose," Ulrich mumbled, but he didn't look too happy.

Claire gave him her most dazzling smile. "I can have that information to you tomorrow morning, Dr. Ulrich."

"Very well."

He left her office shaking his head. Not until he was out the door did her tension begin to dissipate. Waiting until her pulse steadied and she was certain Ulrich wasn't going to pop back in on her, Claire turned off the screen saver and entered the next number.

Mac Ellroy had worked in Lab 7, too. When he'd called to tell her about the job opening for Supervisor of Computer Services, he'd hinted that the Project Cypress experiment was something he'd never imagined working on, but he'd kept his oath of secrecy as to content. And then only a few days after she'd interviewed for the job, he'd disappeared. Luckily she hadn't used Mac as a reference or she wouldn't have been offered the position.

The official story was that the lab tech hadn't liked the isolation of St. Stephens, so that he'd quit, moved back to Washington.

But if he had come back to D.C., the first thing Mac would have done was demand she meet him at their favorite wine bar for a spill-all. He hadn't told her he was going anywhere. His land phone had gone out of service, and he wasn't answering his cell or returning her messages. His landlord here in St. Stephens had said he'd gotten notice of Mac's leaving via an e-mail. Supposedly, Mac had simply cleared out and had left an extra month's rent on the kitchen counter.

In cash.

Nothing in Mac's handwriting, not even a check.

Claire had called every mutual friend and acquaintance in D.C., but no one seemed to know where to find him, not even Mac's ex-boyfriend. Benjamin had already moved on to a new lover, and Mac was the last thing on his mind.

But Mac had certainly been on Claire's. Still was every time she looked at the ring she wore on her right hand—the class ring that Mac had bought her as a high-school graduation present because she'd had no money to buy one for herself. They'd joked that their matching rings would bind them together forever.

But now Mac had vanished.

Had he stumbled onto something in the lab that had made it necessary for him to disappear?

Or had someone saved him the trouble?

She wondered, as probably everyone did, about Brayden Sloane, another "missing person." He'd last been seen on the night of the lab accident. Was the security expert in part responsible for the terrible things that had happened at Cranesbrook both before and after the accident?

Or was he yet another victim?

Chapter Two

"If you don't want that, I'll be happy to eat it," a wizened old man said, a wrinkled, blue-veined hand snaking out over one of the two plank tables in the dining room.

His mind had been wandering again, but once awakened to reality, he lowered his arm and prevented the theft.

"If there are leftovers, they'll give you more."

He shoveled in his food—the only way he could think about the stew that filled the hole in his belly. The food was as austere as the facility. In addition to several bedrooms fitted with multiple sets of bunk beds, there was a common room filled with not-so-gently used furniture, this dining hall, three toilets and a shower room.

Though he remembered little more than bits and pieces of his life—not enough to connect the dots—he knew he didn't ordinarily live at this low level.

He remembered the feel of a real bed with a real mattress and the taste of a medium-rare rib eye and the touch of hundreds of needles of water spraying on him from multiple directions at once. He had other memories, too, precipitated by touching various objects, most notably a set of keys that had remained in his pocket. Like a car that was low and fast, a house whose back porch had a water view, an attractive redhead who aggravated him.

What he didn't remember was his name. Or his address. Or where he worked. Nothing that would give him a clue as to his identity.

He could conjure nothing of true significance, no fully fleshed scenario that had taken place before he'd awakened on a boat in the middle of Chesapeake Bay. The owner and his friends hadn't been too happy, especially not with the way he'd looked. One of them had called him a bum.

But at least they hadn't thrown him overboard, and when they'd realized he was hurt, rather than simply dump him at the marina where they'd docked, they'd taken him to an ER and had turned over his wallet to the guy at the intake desk.

Big mistake.

By the time the triage nurse had wheeled him into her cubicle, his wallet had disappeared, and with it any clue as to his identity. Even so, the hospital staff had kept him overnight for observation, sticking him in a bed against the wall in the ER with the other insurance-free indigents.

His mind had worked furiously to grab on to something that would tell him who he was; he hadn't been able to sleep all night.

In the morning, the doc taking care of him said that it might take some time, but most likely memories would start trickling in. The hospital social worker had placed him at this homeless shelter for men. He'd slept, but every night he'd been visited by the recurring nightmare. Maybe there was more wrong with him than a few stitches could fix.

He'd lost count of the days he'd been here as easily as he had of himself. The memories had started coming back, but at a really slow trickle.

"Are you done with your newspaper?" he asked a salt-and-pepper-haired man who sat on the other side of the table.

"Be my guest." The guy shoved it at him. "Nothin' but bad news anyhow."

"Thanks."

As he took the paper, their hands collided, and he was hit with an image of the man very different from the one sitting across from him. The guy wore a hard hat and clung to a metal span high up on an open floor of a building-in-progress. Nausea hit him as though he were afraid of heights, then dissipated as quickly as the image of the construction worker.

His hands trembled as he smoothed the *Baltimore Sun* out in front of him.

What the hell had that been about? It wasn't the first time he'd had an episode like that, either. Touching things had become a chancy proposition. He never knew what was going to pop into his head. Was he going crazy? Is that why he couldn't remember who he was?

He glanced at the date on the paper's masthead and realized he'd been at the shelter for eleven days. How was he ever going to get out of here and back to where he belonged when he couldn't even keep track of time?

His gaze dropped to the lead story. Security Expert Sought For Questioning. Two photos accompanied the article. One of a baby, the other of a man who looked amazingly like the guy in his mirror. Spiked dark hair, pale gray eyes, broad forehead, square jaw.

He really could be the guy in the photo.

His stomach knotted as he skimmed the article.

Brayden Sloane…brother of Echo Sloane…uncle of a kidnapped baby named Zoe…partner in Five Star Security in Baltimore…formerly in charge of security for biggest client, Cranesbrook Associates in St. Stephens, until a mysterious explosion twelve days before…

Twelve days ago, he'd somehow ended up in a boat coming from St. Stephens.

Coincidence?

Brayden Sloane. It seemed to fit. Unable to deny he looked like the man in the photo, he tried on the name. Brayden…Bray. That was it, had to be. Right? At last, he thought he had a name.

What about the rest?

Remembering the second part of the recurring dream—the explosion in a lab, a white-coated man on the floor—he thought that might have happened at this Cranesbrook Associates. But what about the baby? His niece?

He vaguely remembered a round little face, dimpled cheek and a tiny hand that clung to his finger. The thought tightened his chest and he felt anger surge through him that someone would hurt her.

He took a deep breath and tried to remember the past, but no matter how hard he tried, nothing new came to him. Bits and pieces of memory floated around in his brain but he simply had no control over what he could latch on to.

Kind of like the touching thing. Only, those memories belonged to other people.

He finished skimming the article. The authorities were looking for him in connection with both incidents. Did they merely think he had information or did they really think he was a criminal?

Was he? Of what exactly was he guilty?

Bray didn't know.

He couldn't have kidnapped his niece, though. When she'd gone missing, he'd been right here at the shelter, as he had since being released from the ER.

As to the incident at Cranesbrook, he simply didn't know his own involvement. That lack of knowledge being the stumbling block to turning himself in. What if they locked him up for good? Then he might never know what really happened.

First he needed to find out more. The truth. See if he could jump-start his memory. To do that, he would have to get to St. Stephens. To Cranesbrook itself.

But how? In addition to the set of keys in his pocket, he'd found some bills and change. A little less than twenty bucks. He'd spent nearly five already. Not to mention he didn't know where he was going.

Approaching the volunteer at the food table, a soft-looking, middle-aged woman, easy to talk to, he asked, "Hey, Sophie, can you tell me where St. Stephens is?"

"Across the Chesapeake, honey."

"Any way to get there other than by boat?"

"Sure. You could drive down through Annapolis and take the bridge over. Well, if you had a car. I don't know if a bus goes across the Chesapeake or not. Did you remember something, honey? Do you know who you are, where you belong?"

"I only wish. Thanks, Sophie."

He did have keys to a car, only he didn't know where he'd stashed the vehicle. Maybe in St. Stephens. And he wouldn't have the bucks for a bus anyway. That left only one option he could count on.

He wondered how long it would take his thumb to get him where he needed to be.

STILL AT HER COMPUTER, Claire entered another number…another…and another….

She spent all afternoon wasting her time on what proved to be a futile task.

The whole time, her mind kept spinning, kept looking for reasons why people associated with the mysterious Project Cypress weren't safe.

Her worst fear was that her best friend had been the first one to die because of it. And then his death had been covered up. A *professional* cover-up, she thought. The reason she'd still taken the job at Cranesbrook when it had been offered to her.

The only reason she'd applied for something so far from D.C. in the first place had been to be near Mac. She'd been lonely and had wanted to be near the only person who really felt like family to her.

And now he was gone and others were dead, and a mystery shrouded the two owners of Five Star Security in particular.

Her thoughts strayed to Gage Darnell, Brayden Sloane's partner. Gage had been affected by the lab explosion, had been taken to Beech Grove Clinic along with Wes Vanderhoven. But unlike Vanderhoven, who was still there for all she knew, Gage had escaped.

She didn't get that part—why he'd needed to escape the clinic as if he'd been held prisoner.

Suddenly it hit her—the significance of the wire transfer that had gone from Cranesbrook to a Dr. Morton at the clinic the morning after the explosion. She'd seen it by accident, really, and had thought nothing of the money that had changed businesses. Only she was thinking of it now.

Two million bucks for what?

She switched gears and ran a search on Beech Grove Clinic but found no documents that pertained to the accident or to the men brought there or to the money.

Cover-up money?

Unable to find the entry, she tried again. No dice. Nothing. It was gone. Poof. As though it had never existed.

Cover-up money covered up?

Frustrated, Claire gave up for the moment. Tired of entering numbers that didn't work and checking files that had no answers for her, she felt as if she would never solve anything from her desk. The next step, then, was to see if she could find any answers in Lab 7 itself now that it had been cleared.

Answers the authorities hadn't been able to find.

She sighed.

She didn't even know what she was looking for. She only knew she had to try.

THUMBING FOR RIDES didn't work nearly as efficiently as a steering wheel and an accelerator, Bray soon learned. For one, the average citizen was wary of picking up a stranger. Truck drivers were far more accommodating, perhaps because they spent too many hours alone in their cabs.

He'd picked up his easiest ride down to Annapolis. The driver had offered him gum, and in taking a piece, Bray had seen the guy with a group of little kids surrounding him as he handed out sticks of gum from a big pack.

Getting across the bridge that spanned the Chesapeake was a bit trickier. So was the driver. Bray didn't get anything off him until his map got knocked to the floor and the driver asked Bray if he could get it. Suddenly, Bray was driving through a desert of saguaro cactus and figured the guy was a long way from home.

Heading south along the eastern shore had been the big problem. No eighteen-wheelers going his way. Only lots of suspicious drivers. He'd managed it, though, walking maybe a third of the way.

Finally he'd caught a ride with an older woman who had two dogs big enough to tear him to bits if he made a wrong move. Patting one of them, he saw the dog on his back, wiggling like a puppy for his mistress, who was wearing a smile she apparently saved for her pets. Without so much as a change of expression, she'd let him off at the edge of town.

So here he was, hours later, approaching Cranesbrook on foot.

The sun had set and deep shadows gave the place an added spooky feel as darkness fell. Ahead, chain-link fence topped by razor wire surrounded several red brick buildings. A security station was set up at the entrance and a guard in gray was checking incoming vehicles.

Bray clung to the side of the road where his approach could be hidden by clusters of bushes and trees. He watched intently, but didn't see the guard glance his way as he checked in a car and then a van. A supply truck rumbled down the lane and as it passed Bray, a cigarette butt flicked out of the window and landed at his feet, as if he were meant to pick it up. So he did.

Immediately he saw the driver and the uniformed guard chatting away like old buddies....

Maybe they were. And maybe that would give him a way into the compound, Bray thought, noting the back of the truck was only half-gated.

Some buried instinct took over and he seamlessly slipped through the shadows as the truck came to a stop.

"Hey, Johnny, kinda late for a delivery," he heard the guard say.

"Hormones, Howard, hormones. They get a man right where he lives."

Bray ducked low and, without making a sound, crossed to the back of the delivery truck.

"New woman, huh?" the guard asked as Bray found a toehold for a boost upward.

"Nothing permanent. Met her in that new nudie bar up on the highway. She's on her way west. Needed someplace to stay last night."

Lightly hauling himself over the gate, Bray noted how familiar this felt to him, as if his body was trained for this kind of activity. His pulse had quickened but that was the only effect the subterfuge had on him.

"So you gave it to her?" the guard asked.

"I gave it to her, all right—all night!"

The two men laughed lewdly as Bray settled down among bushes and small trees. The truck was filled with landscaping materials. Manure included. Catching his breath against the permeating odor, he decided to wait until the truck passed the main building before ditching it. Suddenly he realized he knew the landscaping office was in a building on the other side of the grounds.

An honest-to-God new memory that belonged to him rather than someone else!

As the truck started up again, Bray wondered if, once he was inside, all his questions would be answered as easily as he'd gotten into a supposed high-security complex.

Peering out through the branches of a bush, he saw the security station recede and the main building come into view. Out of nowhere came the thought that the building had two wings—one of offices, the other of labs—both facing a little nature preserve with a lake and rock and grasses in the center. If he remembered that much, he might remember more once inside.

Staying low, he crawled to the gate, waiting for the moment the truck would drive through a darkened area and counting on the driver having no need for his rearview mirror.

That would be…

Now!

Bray slid up and over the gate, dropping to his feet

and rolling. He kept rolling off the road into the grass. The truck didn't so much as slow down.

Keeping to the shadows, he got to his feet and, gaze roaming over the open area to make sure no one could surprise him, ran toward the back of the main building and the rear door that had a keypad entry. Another memory that came back to him out of nowhere.

Once inside, would he remember everything?

Would he *get* inside?

It suddenly occurred to him that he might not be able to figure out the security code. The newspaper article had said Five Star Security had been replaced by another company, one that had probably made all kinds of changes.

Not that he actually remembered the code his own company had used—a realization that hit home as he stopped at the back door and stared down at the mechanism.

Now what?

Instinct brought his fingers over the keypad. Tentatively touching it, he nearly jumped out of his skin when a series of numbers whipped through his mind. This was just like the images he'd been having all day touching objects that belonged to other people.

Their memories?

Or was he simply out of his mind?

One way to find out. He quickly entered the numbers on the keypad.

Click.

The door opened.

He was in.

CLAIRE WAITED UNTIL the end of the day to go poking around Lab 7. It wasn't unusual that she was at Cranesbrook long after the majority of the staff had left. Everyone thought she was so dedicated to her work, when in reality, she was dedicated to finding the key to Mac's disappearance.

Knowing she was outside of her element and playing with fire, she grabbed a folder of information on that new computer program Dr. Ulrich wanted to buy. She swept out of her office with the folder under her arm as though she meant to deliver it to Ulrich, who'd left his office a while ago.

At least that was what she would tell the director of research if she ran into him.

Claire knew she could convince anyone of anything. When you came from a family where no one told the truth on a regular basis, you learned to spin a good tale at an early age. The ability to make a lie sound like reality was something she was good at, right up there with her computer skills.

No one was inside the suite, but the door wasn't locked, either, which meant Ulrich was still somewhere on the complex premises. Where he might be, she didn't know, but she was going to wing it.

Knowing he had to have an extra set of keys to the labs, she quickly searched his assistant's desk. Marge was a nice woman with a relaxed attitude, something Claire was counting on. Sure enough, the assistant had left a ring of keys at the back of her top desk drawer. Most of them were marked with a numeral. Two with a 7.

Noting the cuts were different, Claire took them both and tucked the keyring back where she'd found it.

Her heart fluttered as she made her way down the laboratory corridor. So far, so good. No one in attendance. She heard some muffled sounds in some of the labs—voices, a scrape, a crash followed by a curse—but no heads poked from the doorways to see what she was up to.

Standing in front of Lab 7's door, Claire felt her stomach tighten and churn. The door was soot-stained, looking worse for the wear, but it was closed. Probably locked. She reached out, took a big breath, then tested the handle, expecting she would have to use the key. She didn't. That it turned made her more nervous. Was someone already inside? Ulrich?

Her fingers tightened around the folder. She pasted a smile to her lips—just in case she had to use her cover story—and opened the door.

The lab was dark.

Shoulders sagging with relief, Claire stepped inside and pulled the door closed behind her. No doubt the lab was open because Project Cypress had just been moved and someone figured you didn't need to lock an empty lab.

A little light came in through the windows that faced the center of the Cranesbrook campus with its lake surrounded by rocks and natural grasses. No one ever went out there—not that she had ever seen—but anyone in the wing across the way could see into the lab, as well, a reason not to turn on the room lights until she'd closed the blinds. Circling a lab table, she crossed the room and did so.

That accomplished, she pulled a Maglite from her pocket, but before she could click it on and sweep the narrow beam through the darkened room, something flitted at the edge of her vision. Her stomach knotted and the breath caught in her throat. What the hell was that? Her pulse thrummed. She stood perfectly still and listened hard for any sound.

Nothing.

Not even the intake of breath.

And yet she knew she wasn't alone.

So what did she do? Switch on the Maglite? Face down the other person? An intruder like herself? Who else would be in the abandoned lab in the dark?

Sensing she'd put herself in danger, Claire decided that the smart thing would be to book out of here as fast as her feet would carry her.

But no sooner did she take a single step than a big body bumped up against her back and a hand covered her mouth. She jammed her elbow backward and got a single "Oof!" in response, but the grip didn't loosen. Though she tried to twist and turn, she couldn't free herself. The folder went flying as she stomped backward but missed her attacker's foot.

He was so damned strong. What was she going to do?

The only thing she could think of.

She let herself go limp, hoping the surprise of her dead weight would make him let go.

Instead he went down with her, crashing to the lab floor. Though she writhed in his arms, the only thing she accomplished was to free one arm and twist around so she was facing him as he landed on top of her.

Shrieking in frustration, Claire snapped on the

Maglite and shone it in his battered, beard-shadowed face.

Her eyes widened and she gasped, "Brayden Sloane, get the hell off me!"

Chapter Three

His touching her wreaked havoc on him. Irritation and attraction warred with one another, and for a moment, even though her face was still in the dark, he clearly saw reddish brows knit together in a frown over annoyed green eyes.

Familiar...

He shook himself and demanded, "You know who I am, right?"

"Of course I know. Now, get off. Please."

Bray picked himself up off the floor. "I didn't hurt you, did I?"

He thrust a hand into the pool of light, but she ignored his offer of help. Instead she scrambled to her feet and, backing away from him, shone that bright light directly into his eyes.

"What are you doing here?" she demanded.

"Trying to get to the truth." She wasn't on the up-and-up herself, he realized, not sneaking around in the dark with a Maglite. He instinctually remembered her if not her name. "What about you?"

"The same."

"You're trying to get to the truth? About what?"

"What happened in here," she said. "The accident, of course."

The lab explosion in his dream. He'd seen it again when he'd touched the door handle. Nearly overpowered by the memory, he'd made it inside the lab. He'd gone shaky for a moment and had stood quietly, trying not to let the memory eat at him, fighting to regain control.

That was when he'd heard the noise outside the door and had prepared himself for an assault. He hadn't meant to be the one doing the assaulting, but he couldn't let her blow the whistle on him, not when he had no answers.

"Maybe we should turn on the room light," he suggested.

"Good idea."

She backed away from him and a few seconds later, light cast a fluorescent glow over the space.

Bray didn't know what he'd expected, but the lab was less threatening than it had been in his dreams. There were signs of something having happened—the door to an inner room was split, hanging crookedly on its hinges, and there were streaks of soot on the nearby walls and tables. But other than that, it simply looked like an empty lab.

The woman put him more on edge than his surroundings. Her red hair waved around her oval face and brushed the shoulders of her navy pantsuit, its starkness offset by a sparkly green scarf and matching shoulder-duster earrings. Her equally green eyes were rounded, and she was biting her full bottom lip as if trying to decide what to do about him.

"You're not thinking about screaming, are you?" he asked as he crossed toward the inner room, sending his gaze into every corner.

"I don't scream."

"Because if you did, you'd get caught."

"I work here."

"Not in this lab," he reminded her as he flicked the inner room light on.

More damage. A table with a broken leg. A couple of shelves that had collapsed. Other than the damaged furniture, the room was empty. He touched the table and was rewarded with a replay of the explosion, of the man in the white lab coat on the floor.

His pulse rushed through his head, filling it with sound, and he barely heard the woman state, "I could say I saw you and followed you."

He whipped around to face her and felt the heat for a second, but he quickly got himself under control.

"Is that a threat?" he snapped, pacing toward her.

She backed up another step. "I—it could be."

Bray could see she was still wary of him but undecided, so he stopped just outside of her personal space and brought the question into the open. "Do you think I did it?"

"What?"

"The lab accident. Do you think I was responsible?"

"Were you?"

He'd tried to grab on to the truth since getting inside, but nothing new had come to him. "I don't know."

"What do you mean, you don't know?"

"Just that. Something happened to me… I must have hit my head pretty good, I guess," he said, "because I don't remember. Not about the accident. Not about anything. That's why I came back."

Expression disbelieving, she asked, "If you have no memory, how did you know to come to Cranesbrook?"

"Today's *Baltimore Sun*. Even I couldn't deny the resemblance when I saw my picture on the front page. Made for some interesting reading, but I don't know what the hell to believe. I thought I would find out for myself, only so far no go."

Her red-rimmed mouth rounded into an O, making Bray wonder what it would feel like under his.

"So you don't remember anything?" she asked a little breathlessly.

"Nothing I can get hold of. Fragments...dreams... visions...whatever you want to call them." Nightmares he couldn't seem to escape. "Nothing substantial. Seeing that article in this morning's paper was the first real breakthrough. I thought maybe by coming here I'd remember something."

"No wonder you just vanished," she murmured, her voice low, as if she were debating what he'd been saying. "People think it's because you're guilty."

"What do *you* think?"

She shrugged. "I don't know for sure, but I'd say not. Unless the straight-arrow act was just that."

"Nice that someone's willing to give me the benefit of the doubt."

"Of course I would." She bit her lip again, then blurted, "You don't remember me at all?"

Just that she annoyed him. Not that he would tell her that. "Vaguely. Sorry."

She took a big breath. "Well, wives give their husbands the benefit of the doubt."

"Wives?" Her statement shook him. "You're saying we're married?" How could he forget such an intimate connection? "I don't even remember your name."

No sooner had she said, "Claire. My name's Claire Fanshaw," than he heard a sound coming from the hallway.

Someone's coming, he mouthed, and indicated she should turn out the room light.

Without hesitation, she hit the wall switch as he grabbed her other hand and pulled her behind the door. His mind was racing as he started to plan what he would do if they were discovered. He could push Claire down and then when the enemy appeared—

What the hell was he thinking? That he would hurt some security guard who was only doing his job? Apparently he was used to violence.

Maybe he *was* guilty.

The footsteps drew closer.

Claire snugged up against him, her derriere to his groin, her silky hair sweeping against his cheek. The sexless suit hid soft curves that, despite the situation, set him on fire. He wanted to groan but he didn't dare make a sound. Instead he froze and sublimated his breath as the footsteps stopped right outside the door.

Stiffening, Claire pressed into him harder but remained equally silent.

The knob rattled and the door swung open and Bray told himself to take it easy, not to hurt anyone. The room light went on. He could hear the man's breathing. The man didn't move, just stood there on the other side of the wooden panel as if he were carefully checking things out.

Damn!

The folder that had flipped out of Claire's hands was on the floor for anyone to see.

Tension wired through Bray, but just when he thought the guard was going to discover them, the light flicked out and the door swung closed. And Claire went limp against him. She was trembling, probably scared out of her wits. Not that she would admit it, he was certain. She had some moxie going for her, he would give her that.

The footsteps receded and silence reigned. And then Claire took a big breath and stepped away from him. Once more the Maglite clicked on.

"Now what?" she asked.

"Now we get out of here."

"But I haven't even looked the place over carefully."

"I looked carefully enough for both of us."

They weren't going to find anything revealing because everything but some furniture had been removed. And he didn't think he was going to get any more of his weird visions than he already had.

Sighing, Claire nodded and crossed to where the folder had landed. "I guess you're right," she said, picking it up and straightening the contents. "There really is nothing here to see anymore. I need to go the front way so I can sign out, or tomorrow someone may question how and why I left without doing so. And the keys. I need to return the keys."

"Do whatever you have to."

"What about you?" she asked.

"I'll get out the same way I got in—through the back door."

"But you needed the code to get in. Ace Security changed it when they took over."

"Okay."

She gave him a look but she didn't try to make him explain how he'd figured out the new code.

"Will you wait for me?" she asked. "I can bring the car around in about ten minutes."

"And raise someone's suspicions? I'll come around to the parking lot and find you."

"You will be there, right? You won't forget?"

"Don't worry, my short-term memory is just fine."

"All right. You probably don't remember what I drive, though. It's a dark blue Honda CRV."

"I'll find it," he assured her, stepping to the door and pressing his ear to the panel.

Nodding, she clicked out her light. He opened the door a crack and peered out. Not so much as a foreign shadow grayed the hallway.

"Clear," he whispered, and gave her the signal to go.

Claire hesitated only a second, as if she wanted to say something to him, then brushed by him as she made her way out.

Bray found himself watching her, appreciating the slight sway of her hips as she sauntered down the hallway like a woman who was simply late on the job.

He shook himself. He couldn't get lax. Couldn't let the enemy have the upper hand.

Even as he scanned the corridor before slipping

toward the exit in the opposite direction, he realized his thinking was inappropriate.

This wasn't the military and there was no enemy here.

STARING OUT OF A WINDOW into the dark, he watched her race across the Cranesbrook parking lot.

Claire Fanshaw. Who the hell was she, really?

A cop? A Fed? Or just an ordinary woman too nosy for her own good?

He'd caught sight of her as she'd taken the lab corridor and, wondering what she'd been up to, he'd followed. Discreetly, of course. And when she'd disappeared, instinct had taken him straight to Lab 7.

She'd been inside.

The moment he'd snapped on the light his gaze had been drawn directly to the folder on the floor. The folder she'd been carrying. It had taken all his will not to let his temper get the best of him. Not to swipe up the folder to see what was in it and demand she show herself. That simply would have been foolish.

First, he needed to know who she was, what she wanted, what she already knew. He needed to know if she was a threat or a minor inconvenience.

The lights of her vehicle flashed as she approached it. A nearby shadow separated in two and the silhouette of a man dressed in khaki raced for the CRV. Even as the shadow-man opened the rear passenger door, he looked toward the building—and the light—just for a second. But a second was long enough to get a quick look at his face.

Brayden Sloane!

What the hell was the former security chief doing on

the grounds? Where had he been for nearly two weeks? What did he know about what had happened in Lab 7?

His stomach cramped and acid reflux soured his mouth. Sloane's reappearing was an unexpected complication. When the security expert had disappeared, he'd assumed the man had gone off and died somewhere. Maybe drowned in Chesapeake Bay, only to be washed up in some remote area at a future date.

He hadn't expected this.

His jaw clenched tight as he helplessly watched the vehicle head for the security station.

He might have believed Claire to be an inconvenience, but Sloane was a liability, one that couldn't go unchecked. And if they were a team, working together against him, they were doubly dangerous to his plans.

He would have to take care of them both.

But first he had an experiment to conduct.

On himself.

Chapter Four

Waving to the security guard as she drove out of the Cranesbrook lot, Claire couldn't believe her own audacity. Bray was scrunched down across the back seat floor, at least half convinced they were man and wife.

What had she been thinking?

She hadn't been. The lie had been a gut reaction, one meant to keep Bray with her so she could get information out of him. She'd even switched her class ring to her left hand, as if it were her wedding ring. Desperation was the mother of creative invention.

Maybe with Bray's help, she could figure out the mystery of Lab 7. Well, not Lab 7 anymore, since Project Cypress had been moved, but the mystery of Mac's sudden disappearance, the thing that drove her, that kept her up at night.

"It's safe to get up now," she said, checking the rearview mirror in time to see Bray sit up.

She considered pulling over to let him get in the front passenger seat. Then revised that idea. She felt more comfortable with a little distance between them. Not that she suspected he would hurt her. But it had been difficult to think clearly with him too close. When they'd hidden behind the lab door while the security guard had checked out the area, Bray's nearness had threatened to suffocate her.

"So where is home?" he asked.

"We're not going home."

"Why not?"

"They might have someone posted, watching for you there." She was making this up as she went along, but it didn't sound too far-fetched, she reasoned.

"They?"

"The authorities are still looking for you as a person of interest."

"Because of Zoe's kidnapping."

Because of what had gone on at Cranesbrook, Claire thought. Everything related back to Project Cypress, starting with Mac's disappearance. "So you remember your niece?"

"Not really. Not in the way you mean."

"How, then?"

"Impressions. Like I'm sure I touched her, held her."

Uh-oh, he wasn't going to have like impressions of *her* and she was supposed to be his wife. "Is that how you remember things?" she asked, trying to keep the concern from her voice. "Simple impressions?"

"Mostly."

How else? Claire wondered. And how long would it be before Bray saw through her pretense?

When she turned onto the main road, he asked, "Where are we headed?"

"For Breezy Cove Marina. I'm taking care of a boat

for some friends. Lainie and John," she added. "The Moores. Sound familiar?"

"Sorry."

Of course the name wouldn't sound familiar since he didn't know the couple. But she had to make their relationship sound convincing. Sometimes it was the small things that counted most in getting another person to relax his guard.

When she'd told Lainie she'd taken a job at Cranesbrook, her old friend had said she could live on the boat until she found an apartment. John's work had taken them to Budapest for six months, so they wouldn't be doing any sailing until next season. The boat would be just sitting there at the marina until it had to go to dry dock.

Which would be all too soon, Claire realized. She'd hoped to have answers—and another job—before this.

"So you work at Cranesbrook?" he asked.

"Supervisor of computer systems. And you were chief of security. That's how we met."

"So we haven't been married long."

"Not long at all." Not wanting to get into exact days or anything, as she'd hardly had time to think this through, she changed the subject to the one that interested her. "About the accident—don't you remember anything?"

"I've been dreaming about it, I think. Noise and confusion and a guy in a lab coat on the floor."

Now they were getting somewhere. Claire gripped the wheel in excitement.

"Wes Vanderhoven," she told him. "He and your partner, Gage Darnell, were taken to Beech Grove Clinic for observation." She waited a moment and said,

"Gage escaped, though. Any idea why he couldn't just sign himself out?"

"Sorry. I don't even remember my partner—what he looks like, his personality, nothing."

Okay, nothing there. Back to the accident.

"So you saw Wes Vanderhoven unconscious on the lab floor. Then what did you do?"

Bray was silent for a moment before saying, "Me? Nothing. There was some kind of explosion from the storeroom."

A fact she already knew. "And then what?"

"I guess that must be when I hit my head."

"So you have no idea how you got out of the lab or Cranesbrook?"

"I told you I didn't remember."

"Not even an impression?"

Bray made a sound of exasperation and said, "Not even an impression!"

"The authorities think you know something," she pressed.

"I'm aware of that from the article in the *Baltimore Sun.* They're wrong. I only wish…" Bray fell silent for a moment, then said, "What kind of husband am I, turning you into a criminal?"

"You can't think that way."

Claire didn't want him going all noble on her and disappearing for her own good. Not before she worked on him some more. He was bound to get his memory back, probably in bits and pieces, and she wanted to be there when anything associated with the lab accident kicked in. Hopefully he would remember that before he remembered her.

"You'll be harboring a fugitive," Bray said grimly.

"You're wanted for questioning, is all. The police aren't out to arrest you."

"You don't know that."

"According to the newspaper article—"

"It's a ruse. Then they get me where they want me and the next thing you know, I'm on trial."

"You sound like you know what you're talking about. Have you been arrested before?"

He hesitated, then said, "I'm not sure. I don't remember."

Bray's uncertainty put a knot in Claire's stomach. She was going on faith that he was the square shooter she'd assumed he was. She didn't need the complication of being up close and personal with a truly dangerous man.

When Breezy Cove Marina came into view, she tried to put away all her reservations. Having access to Bray Sloane was her first real break. She wasn't going to lose him out of fear. Trusting her own instincts had always served her well and she wasn't about to let unfounded doubts change that.

Breezy Cove was an inlet on the Chesapeake less than a mile from St. Stephens. The marina was fairly small. No fancy Olympic-size pools or gazebo. There was a white, red-roofed building that held a café and supply store, a bath house and laundry. A picnic area had a covered pavilion and a small playground for kids. A half dozen docks held nearly two hundred seasonal slips, and there was a separate dock for transient boats. A fuel station and a maintenance area were located at one end of the marina, the parking lot at the other.

Lainie's Moor was docked near the parking lot, so the transfer from land to water was quick and private. This late in the season, few people were around after dark anyway. As far as Claire knew, no one else slept on any of the other boats except for an overnighter, usually on a weekend.

The boat itself was a fiberglass thirty-four-footer with a bow pulpit and rail, three-quarter flybridge enclosure and a hardtop. Inside, the galley was equipped with a refrigerator, burners, microwave and dinette.

Claire led the way inside the cabin, slipping out of her suit jacket and scarf and throwing them and her briefcase on the dinette bench.

"It's kind of cramped in here," Bray said, glancing up at the ceiling that sat mere inches from the top of his spiked black hair.

He was a big man for such a small space, tall, with broad shoulders. Claire imagined that beneath the long khaki shirt sleeves, his arms were muscled like steel.

Releasing the breath that caught in her throat, she said, "Think of it as cozy."

"Do you always see the glass half full?"

"Do you always see it half empty?" she countered.

"You tell me."

He was challenging her. Because it amused him or because he didn't quite believe she knew him well enough to be his wife? She read people quite accurately, though, and she had come up against him a few times at work.

"You take things super-seriously, Bray. Life. Yourself. You see things in black and white. Right and wrong. You have a pretty intimidating scowl."

"You don't seem intimidated."

He was scowling at her now. She was a little intimidated but she wouldn't show it. She could bluff the best of them.

"That's because I'm your match, I guess."

One of his dark brows lifted. "My opposite?"

"You could say that."

"Does that mean you *don't* take things seriously? That you *don't* see things in black or white? That you're *not* a straight arrow?"

She couldn't have described herself more accurately. "Opposites attract and all that." Though she felt caught, she kept her voice light.

"That's what they say."

Claire breathed more easily as he broke eye contact and continued looking around. "Good thing I'm not claustrophobic. I'm not, am I?"

"I'm not sure we've ever had the opportunity to find out."

"Well, here it is."

Bray was standing in the doorway, facing the rear of the boat, and Claire knew he was staring at the full-size bed that she'd left unmade. Heat seared her as she thought about bunking with him in that small space. She hadn't quite thought this thing through.

"You need a good night's rest, so you can have the bed," she offered, as if she were simply being reasonable. "I can bunk on the dinette couch."

He eyed the narrow alternative. "I wouldn't think of kicking my wife out of bed."

It was then she knew he was playing her. Somehow she had kicked up his suspicions. What had she said, done wrong?

Then it dawned on her.

Rather, what *hadn't* she done?

Uh-oh.

Knowing how to fix this, Claire forced a smile to her lips and swayed toward Bray as though it were the most natural thing in the world, when what she really wanted to do was to run the other way.

"I didn't get to say this before, darling, but I'm so relieved you're all right." She slipped her hands up his chest slowly enough to feel his heartbeat accelerate. "I couldn't imagine what happened to you. Why didn't you call me in nearly two weeks?"

He stopped the progression of her hands by cuffing her wrists with his fingers. He was staring at her left hand. "That's your wedding ring? And I don't wear one?"

"We were in such a rush, we didn't have time to ring shop. So I just used my class ring temporarily."

To distract him, she pushed her hands up until he let go of her wrists. Circling her arms around his neck brought her in full body contact with him. Again. He stirred to life against her belly and she steeled herself against her physical response.

Suddenly breathless, she forced out, "Your memory will come back. You'll see."

When she stood on tiptoe, it was simply to brush her lips over his. A promise of a kiss. Of more intimate things to come in the future.

Bray had other ideas.

Arms like bands of steel wrapped around her waist and wedged her into him. His mouth opened and covered hers, his tongue invading her warmth. For a moment Claire stiffened and thought to fight him, but that would surely convince him she wasn't who she said she was. So she softened against him and let him have his way with her.

It was only a kiss, after all.

And what a kiss. His tongue explored every crevice of her mouth, his teeth plucked at her lower lip, his beard-stubbled face whisked against the soft flesh of her cheek. Claire's pulse raced and her head went light and, without thinking about the consequences, she kissed him with equal fervor.

She hadn't been so attracted to a man in…well, probably never.

Claire had always played the safe card when it came to men. She'd seen the kind of macho creeps her mom had attracted, and early on she'd promised herself that wouldn't be the way she would live her life. Apparently safe translated to lukewarm attraction. She'd taken what she could get in the way of safe relationships, but she'd always thought there should be more—more chemistry, more heat, more love—between a man and a woman than she'd experienced.

Bray's hands slid lower, opening so his palms scooped up her derriere and brought her more solidly in contact with him. Her knees grew weak and she clung to him.

No matter that she knew she ought to stop this now, ought to divert his attention somehow, Claire simply couldn't bring herself to stop the powerful sensations that Bray created in her. Her thighs spread slightly so that her still-clothed center pressed against his length. He moaned and slid his hands down her buttocks and between her thighs so he could open and lift her.

She wrapped her legs around his thighs. Bray started backing up toward the bed. Now would be the time to stop him. *Now.* Before this went any further. And when he came up for air, she tried to find the words to put a halt to this madness. Before she could do so, his head lowered and his mouth nuzzled at her breast through her blouse and she was lost.

Throwing back her head, Claire let sensation wash over her as he nipped at her nipple and suckled it through the material. The sensation was so powerful, she thought she might come without going any further. Then they were moving faster.

Back…back…she was falling backward…and he was falling on top of her.

They landed on the bed, Bray on top, his mouth still pleasuring her breast. The bed swayed with the boat, rocking them closer. Claire felt his hands between them, opening her slacks, tugging the material low on her hips. She wanted to do the same to him, but she couldn't quite reach, so instead she encouraged him by digging her fingernails into his back. That was all it took for him to slide lower, his mouth trailing a pattern down the front of her, his lips sliding against exposed stomach flesh.

Hands shaking, she began unbuttoning her blouse, unhooking her front-clasp bra, but for the moment, he had other interests. He rolled her slacks and panties down over her hips and thighs, his mouth following. Realizing what he was about to do, Claire opened her eyes and watched his dark head descend until his mouth reached the juncture of her softness, and his tongue licked the pooled fluid there.

His tongue entered her, his mouth surrounded her.

Lost… She was lost in a sea of sensation.

Allowing her eyes to close, she stroked herself from stomach to breasts, then surrounded the flesh and rubbed her nipples to double the pleasure. He pushed two fingers hard inside her, lifting her hips from the bed. He eased the fingers out slowly, all the while using his tongue and teeth cunningly on her tender flesh. Sparked by the increasing pressure, she moved against him, lifting her legs, making him drive his fingers deeper into her.

Her head went light and a low moan issued from her throat as the pressure built, but before he completed her, he stopped and she felt him move up the bed. She opened her eyes to see his face over hers. And then she was filled with him, not his fingers, but a more satisfying hardness.

He grabbed her wrists and pulled her hands from her breasts up over her head. He kissed her and she tasted herself on his lips, his tongue. She wanted to touch him, to run her hands over every inch of his skin, but he held her firm, a prisoner of her own desire.

And then he began to move in her. Slowly.

Too slowly.

She pushed against him, snaked her legs around his thighs. The pressure began to build in her, but he didn't seem in any hurry, so she lifted her legs higher, opening herself wider to him so he would lose himself in her.

He moaned and finally she felt him lose that tight control. He moved in her deeper, harder, faster. Little noises escaped her throat as he rode her and the pressure inside her seemed too sharp and yet endless.

"Now!" she whispered, her lips at his ear. She lowered her mouth and nipped the soft flesh of his neck.

He cried out and stiffened and she pushed up her hips as forcefully as she could. That did it. The second his wet warmth began to fill her, she spilled over the edge with him, coming hard and long.

He collapsed against her, still inside her. Drunk with pleasure, she loved the feel of him. And she finally got to touch him, stroke him, imagine what more sex with him would be like.

The sex-fever seemed to take forever to dissipate, but when it did, cold reality began to set in.

Claire could hardly believe what she'd done. She was no innocent, but normally she at least knew and cared for a guy before sleeping with him. Bray Sloane was a virtual stranger and she'd lied to him about being his wife.

Normally she didn't believe in guilt, she simply hadn't been raised to worry about what she told people. But for once in her life, Claire was shaken enough to feel real guilt that she'd gone further than she should have to fool Bray into believing they were a couple.

Worse, she was supposed to be figuring out what happened to her best friend, not sleeping with someone who could be the enemy.

Bray's hand moving on her breast and his fingers playing with her nipple distracted her from that thought.

"What, you're not asleep?" she asked.

"Is that what I usually do?"

A rhetorical question.

He didn't wait for an answer, hooked a hand around

the back of her neck and pulled her head to his for a deep, arousing kiss that momentarily superceded doubt.

HE'D SWEAR he'd never had sex with this woman before.

Surely he would remember if he had. That thought entered Bray's mind the moment he awoke. Claire was curled up against him, all warm and soft. She made little noises in her sleep. Noises that set him off, made him want to wake her and have sex with her a fourth time. He hadn't been able to get enough of her. Nor she of him, apparently.

Instead he slid out of bed. He needed a phone. Entering the galley, he waited a few seconds for his eyes to adjust to the minimal light coming through the boat's windows, then went straight for the jacket she'd dumped on the dinette seat. Sure enough, a search of her pockets produced a cell phone. He headed up top so the fresh air could clear his head first.

The night's fall chill pebbled his flesh, but he was running hot, both body and thoughts, and his body adjusted. With no one around to see him he stood naked on the flybridge, staring out over the quiet marina. The walkways were lit, but the building and the boats themselves remained dark. Not a sound to indicate anyone else was within earshot.

He knew Claire Fanshaw, of that he was certain. Snatches of memories—mostly of them arguing—told him so. He simply wasn't convinced that she was his wife. Her not acting wifely to start could have been situational, he supposed. But not remembering the curves of her body, the throaty noises she made, the way her mouth felt around him—that was what bothered him. It all felt new, like uncharted territory.

Forcing his mind back, he tried to conjure images of making love to a woman. He came up with vague impressions of his enjoying a woman's body, but the woman was smaller, and a blonde rather than a redhead. Who the hell was she? He was caught for a moment, thinking the blonde must have been someone important to him, but he couldn't take the thought to the next step.

And what reason would Claire have to lie? If he was potentially some villain, why would she have done her damnedest to be alone with him? Could they have been married without having sex?

Or maybe he was expecting too much of himself and looking for shadows where there were none. It was a bit much thinking he should remember the texture of this woman's skin when he didn't remember much of anything else.

Trying to get Claire out of his head, Bray flipped open the cell and was relieved when he got a strong signal. He checked the time—11:08—and contacted directory assistance.

"City and state, please," came an impersonal voice.

"Maryland. St. Stephens. Echo Sloane."

Thankfully his sister was listed. Bray repeated the number to himself as the call went through. Tension tightened his muscles as the phone rang.

Once…twice…three times…

Finally the connection was made.

But when a man's voice said, "Sloane residence," Bray's grip on the phone tightened. He almost asked for Echo, but something told him not to say a word.

Gut instinct made him flip the phone closed and turn it off instead.

He didn't remember whether or not his sister had a boyfriend. The man who'd answered had sounded terse. Official. Of course the authorities would be involved because of the kidnapping.

Not that he even knew what he'd meant to say to Echo if he'd been able to talk to her.

A stab in the dark—that was all it had been.

That was all he was doing. Stabbing in the dark. Trying to figure out who the hell he really was. He knew his name now and what he was supposed to do for a living. But beyond that, he was a blank.

As was Claire Fanshaw.

HE RIDES HER as though he can outrun his memories.

"Yeah, baby, that's it," the blonde says in a breathy voice. "I'm almost home."

He holds her hands over her head and looks into her face, concentrating on the tilted blue eyes and full lips. If anyone can make him forget, she can. With a cry, she comes in a sexual explosion....

The kid explodes like a child's piñata, body bursting into bits of flesh and bone.

He loses it, screams like a banshee and runs to the Humvee. His gorge in his throat, he throws himself into the passenger seat, his driver buddy's tortured-sounding curses ringing in his ears.

An explosion inside his head takes away his breath.

His brain is on fire.

Burning. Melting.

He forces back the flames only to have a second flash of sound open his eyes.

A wall of heat engulfs him. Amid rubble and smoke,

a white lab-coated body lies there at his feet. Not the kid. A different explosion, a different victim...

"YOU'RE OKAY. Bray, wake up. You're having a bad dream."

With a gasp, he sat straight up and looked into worried eyes. "Claire."

"You were making terrible-sounding noises." She reached out and touched his face with a gentle hand.

His sleeping with her had brought back another memory. The woman in the dream had been the blonde rather than her. What did the blonde have to do with the explosions?

"Can I get you something?" she asked, looking lovely as a hint of moonlight from the window dappled her nude body. "Tea? Water? Tequila?"

"You."

He reached for her and she rolled into his arms as though she belonged there, and for the next half hour, he forgot that he questioned whether or not she was really his wife.

Chapter Five

Early the next morning, Claire showered, then dressed for work in a rust bouclé suit, a sparkly amber pin in the lapel, matching earrings in her lobes. She'd already written a note for Bray, telling him to stay put, rest and eat, that she would try to get off work early.

She still couldn't believe she'd slept with him. More accurately, had sex with him throughout half the night. What was wrong with her? How could she have let herself get sucked into this?

It had all started with a lie.

Not that it was all that different from other kinds of lies that people told every day—lies meant to spare feelings and to smooth things over as she'd had to do so many times growing up. Her mother had been an alcoholic, and her father hadn't even been a factor in her life. He'd gone missing before she'd been born. Maybe he didn't even know about her. She and her sister and brother all had different fathers, none of whom had stuck around long enough to marry their mother.

Starting at the age of three, Claire remembered being taught to cover for Mom's drinking. The small lies had led to bigger ones. By high school, she'd invented an entire fantasy life for herself that she'd fed to her teachers and friends, because she hadn't wanted anyone feeling sorry for her. If they'd seen through her self-protective storytelling, they'd been kind enough not to let on.

Sometimes Claire thought her whole life had been a lie, but that was the only way she'd been able to survive a dreadful home life.

And maybe now, too.

The question was, how was she going to get out of any further intimacy with Bray?

She couldn't keep having sex with him. Couldn't look Bray straight in the face in daylight without his knowing. Couldn't allow herself any more weakness. She had to keep her mission in mind.

Had to remember she was in this for Mac.

Not to mention Bray, who might truly be a victim in all this. What was she doing to him? Why did she care? Claire wondered. She wasn't hurting him physically. Her pretending to be his wife might even keep him from being behind bars for a while longer.

So why was she feeling guilty about lying to him?

Contemplating that maybe she hadn't chosen the best path in convincing Bray that she was his wife, Claire put the finishing touches to her makeup. There. Now she was ready to leave for Cranesbrook. She was just retrieving her cell phone when she heard footfalls reverberate on the wood planks outside the boat.

Who in the heck was that? No one else had been around this early in the morning. Had someone come looking for her? If anyone came inside, it would be evident that she was hiding what the police had deemed to be a person of interest.

Not good.

Taking a quick peek at Bray, she saw he was still asleep, a sheet twisted through his legs, leaving one hip nude.

Ignoring the bubbly feeling seeing him like that gave her, she grabbed her briefcase and popped out of the cabin and up to the deck.

"Excuse me, Ms. Fanshaw."

"Can I—" She focused on the man on the dock dressed in a navy suit brightened by a red tie. Her stomach lurched. "Detective McClellan."

"Echo and I stopped by to see what you called about last night."

Called? About to protest she hadn't made any such call, she chewed on her lower lip, then adopted a practiced smile for Rand. No doubt she had Bray to thank for this visit. He must have gotten to her cell phone while she slept.

"I just wanted to know how the investigation was going."

"Why not call my cell phone, then? You called Echo."

"I mislaid your card." Thankfully she was quick-witted and these small untruths came easily to her. "But I knew with Echo's baby missing, she'd probably be able to get in touch with you for me." The smile dropped from her lips and she focused on Bray's sister, a pretty woman with streaked brown hair, wearing a gauzy top and hip-hugger jeans. Claire really did feel genuine sympathy for Echo's plight. "Besides, I wanted to tell you how sorry I am to hear what you're going through."

"Thanks."

"It still seems strange to me that you would call Echo for an update on the case," Rand said. "Especially since the two of you haven't met."

Worrying that Bray might wake up at any time and wander up to the deck, Claire checked the steps leading to the boat's cabin. "That's what telephone directories are for."

But Rand still didn't seem to be buying her excuse. "I think you found out something," he said. "Something you're not eager to share with the police."

She glanced down at her watch and noted it was an hour earlier than normal. "Um, I'm going to be late for work."

"You're going to be even later if you have to make a stop at the State Police Barracks."

"All I did was make a phone call."

"And hang up when I answered."

"I didn't know it was you. I didn't know who it was."

"If you were trying to reach me through Echo, why would hearing my voice surprise you?"

"I thought I would just talk to her, tell her how sorry I was and everything. Besides, I've been tense."

"About what?"

Claire looked around again, saying, "If you don't mind, I don't really want my neighbors to know my business."

A good enough excuse. Believable. How would he know there were no neighbors this late in the season?

Echo stepped up next to Rand and touched Claire's forearm. "If you know something, anything, please…"

"I really have to get to work." Claire glanced back at the boat. "Walk with me to my car."

She needed to get them away from the dock, away from the possibility of discovering Bray, so she started for the parking lot. They fell in, one on either side of her.

Waiting until they'd cleared the dock and were crossing the blacktopped parking lot, she said in a low voice, "I don't have any proof."

"Of what?" Rand prodded.

Oh, boy, she hoped she didn't blow it. She was going to give Rand what she knew for certain. "I saw a money transfer. It was put through the day of the accident in Lab 7."

"A money transfer? From Cranesbrook?"

She nodded. "To Dr. Morton at the Beech Grove Clinic. Isn't that where that murder happened?"

Rand nodded. "What was the dollar amount on the transfer?"

"Two mil."

"Two million dollars?" Echo asked, her voice filled with shock.

"Cranesbrook deals in large transactions all the time, but most of them aren't to medical facilities. I'm not sure why it went to a doctor rather than to the clinic itself."

"So why didn't you mention this earlier?" Rand asked.

"Just because a transfer like that isn't common doesn't mean it's not on the up-and-up. Besides, I shouldn't be sharing Cranesbrook financial records."

"So why are you sharing this information now?" Echo asked.

Claire paused, then said, "Because I noticed it, um, disappeared."

"The record of the transfer disappeared?" Rand looked disbelieving. "When?"

"Yesterday. Normally, I wouldn't have thought much of it since I work with the computers, not accounting." She wasn't going to admit she'd been prying through records trying to find answers to the puzzle of Project Cypress. "But with that murder at the clinic, the whole thing struck me as strange."

Excitement beamed from Echo's gray eyes. "They say you can't fully erase files off a hard drive."

Claire shook her head. "You can't."

"Can you get a warrant for those computers?" Echo asked Rand. "Prove they paid big bucks to the clinic to hold those men against their will?"

Exactly the conclusion she'd come to, Claire thought.

"I'm afraid Cranesbrook is off limits," Rand said.

"Off limits?" Claire frowned. "Who told you that?"

"The federal government. As a detective with the state police, my hands are tied."

His brain felt like it was burning.

He'd had a bitch of a headache since waking up on the lab floor at daybreak. At first, he'd been disoriented, feeling as if he were trying to see through a thick, wavering fog. Unsteady when he got to his feet, he'd reached for the lab table to hold himself upright, and his hand had trembled uncontrollably. The worst had been his stomach; he now had a new understanding of projectile vomiting.

That had been a while ago. He'd sat and waited for the effects to go away. Other than the headache, he felt better now. At least he could see where he was going and could walk a straight line. Thankfully there was nothing left in his stomach to reject.

How long had he been out?

He pulled the cell phone from his pocket. Checking the date and time gave him a sense of relief. It had a been a matter of hours—a little more than seven—rather than days. Adjusting the formula downward had lessened the negative effects as he'd hoped it would. His only hesitation had been the thought of spending time in some loony bin the way Darnell and Vanderhoven had.

Vanderhoven. The lab tech had been lording it over him, acting like the power to amplify emotion made the little prick a god. Vanderhoven had been threatening, had declared himself a full partner. Outrageous. That wasn't going to wash. And the unexpected human reactions to the agent opened up a new world of possibilities. Rather than killing people, he could control.

That had done it for him. He'd been unable to resist trying out the formula on himself.

Suddenly he realized early bird employees could show up at any time. And even though he'd sequestered himself in the lab farthest down the corridor, one not currently in use because it was scheduled for upgrading, there was no sense in taking unnecessary chances. Wouldn't do to leave the vials and equipment out where someone could question him. He'd had enough of that problem.

He stared at the vial holder and willed it to rise on its own. But nothing on the table so much as trembled.

Gage Darnell could do it, right? The security chief could lift anything, make anything work with his mind. Even a couple of the damn monkeys could do it.

Then why not him?

He tried again…and again…and yet again to no avail.

Vanderhoven hadn't been gifted with telekinesis, either. Instead the lab tech could make people feel things, bring up their emotional levels. He'd thought it had been a blip in the experiment, but maybe the chemicals worked differently on different minds. That had been difficult to tell when they'd done the experiment on the lab rats.

Did the differences in result have something to do with the differences in their brain function? In their DNA? How soon would he know if the experiment worked on him in any way?

What if he'd used too little of the cocktail?

Angry at his failure to see a change in himself, he gathered together the evidence by hand and put everything away.

What the hell good was Project Cypress if he couldn't count on the results? It hadn't seemed to work on all the monkeys in the same way, either. Maybe he needed to increase the amount taken. Then again, his head was still throbbing viciously. More might have done permanent damage.

Damn, he was disappointed. He'd been counting on the experiment working the way he'd envisioned it. Results equaled monetary rewards. Not that he was greedy, but what they'd come up with was far more valuable than what they'd been paid to produce.

That was why they'd had a change of plans.

Exiting the storeroom, he nearly stepped in his own

vomit. He'd forgotten about the floor. He shouldn't have to clean that mess up himself. That was what janitors were for. Opening the door to the hall, he spotted an elderly Serbian worker in a gray jumpsuit mopping the floor at the other end.

"You. Artur. Over here. And bring your bucket and mop."

"Okay, okay."

Did the janitor have to be so slow? he wondered, thinking it was taking the man forever to get down the hallway with his cleaning tools. Or was it the effects of the chemicals making him feel like Artur was moving in slow motion?

It seemed to him the only effect of the experiment was to make him sick.

The janitor stopped in front of him and waited.

"Not here. In there!" Was the man stupid? "The floor. Clean the damn floor!"

Artur dragged his bucket inside the lab and made a face. "What you have to eat last night?"

"That's none of your business. If you don't want to lose your job, get to work!"

"I work. Okay."

With each exchange, his temper rose. And when the janitor began to mumble to himself while mopping up the mess, he felt his anger rise once more.

"Shut up!"

He had to stop Artur from talking. Not just now. But later. Surely the janitor would tell someone he'd been sick all over the floor. What would stop him? A bribe? But Artur didn't speak English all that well and might miss some of the nuances. Besides, Artur would still know.

The more he thought about it, the angrier he became. The angrier he became, the more his brain felt as if it was burning inside his skull.

He began to pace and glanced outside to the water feature in its natural setting just in time to see a bird of prey swoop down and grab a baby rabbit.

Too bad Artur couldn't get swooped up like that. Maybe get pecked to death and eaten by a vulture. That would shut him up. A couple of buzzards would get rid of the evidence, he thought grimly.

He could almost see it happening.

A distressed sound from the janitor snapped him to. Artur was jabbering, backing up, tripping over his own bucket as a bird of prey swooped down on him.

Startled, heart pounding, he backed into the wall as the bird's beak ripped into the man in front of his eyes. His own emotions shifted from anger to fear for himself, and suddenly the buzzard dissipated like a hologram switched off.

"Artur?"

The man didn't move.

As his vitals steadied and he pushed himself away from the wall, he realized his problem might just have been solved.

Stooping next to the janitor, he felt for a pulse and was elated when he found none. Old Artur's heart had just stopped beating. Just like that. He'd been scared to death by a mentally projected image.

So his experiment had worked, after all, he thought, if not in the way he'd been expecting.

Then he wondered what Claire Fanshaw most feared.

Chapter Six

The idea that the state police had been shut out of Cranes-brook bothered Claire the entire drive to work. The Feds had taken over. Supposedly. Only as far as she knew, one investigation wasn't replacing the other. No one had been around to speak to her, at any rate. And she hadn't heard any rumors, either. It was as though the Feds knew what had happened. Or they didn't…and didn't care.

Could it be that Project Cypress was too important to let anyone stop it from going to completion?

How was she ever going to figure it out? Claire wondered as she drove through the security station and parked. She had Bray, who had no memory. But if he had been involved, that information was imbedded somewhere in his brain.

Could that have been the source of his nightmare?

She was getting out of her car when she heard a siren. Her heart lurched as she spotted an ambulance racing from around back toward the security station.

Another accident?

Grabbing her briefcase, she hurried inside the building to find out.

"You're here early, Miss Fanshaw," the security guard on duty noted.

"I have some catch-up work to do."

"With the hours you work, you surely deserve some time off. And a raise."

"Thanks," she murmured, then switched to her biggest fear. "About that ambulance I just saw—was there another accident? What's going on?"

"No, no accident. One of the janitors had a heart attack about a half hour ago."

"Which one?"

"Artur. You know, the old guy."

"Oh, right." Her pulse steadied. "I'm so sorry. Is he expected to make it?"

The guard shook his head. "They couldn't revive him. He was back in Lab 12 away from everyone." And then, as if expecting she didn't know about Lab 12, he added, "Lab 12 is one of the labs to be updated, so no one goes back there."

Then why had Artur been cleaning it? Claire wondered. "Amazing someone found him so soon."

"Good thing Hank Riddell went back to the storeroom to get something."

The guard's voice changed slightly. Claire figured he didn't like the research fellow, who spoke to the security guards as if they were beneath him.

"Oh. Well, I'd better get to my office, then," she said, giving the guard a smile as she stepped off.

Surely, Artur's death had nothing to do with Project Cypress, though. Old men had heart attacks.

She hurried along the corridor, wishing she could

find the SD chip to get her into the Project Cypress files so she could get out of this place.

Her trying to get clearance to get into the files had been the source of her tension with Bray, who'd refused outright.

Had he known what was in those computer files?

Had he been somehow responsible for whatever had gone wrong in Lab 7?

Even though part of her didn't believe it, the thought plagued her with doubt about herself, her own judgment, her willingness to bed a man she really didn't know. Dark thoughts swirled in her mind as she entered her office and stopped dead at the sight in front of her.

A white lab-coated back was toward her, bent over her desk. Her stack of folders on top was awry and he was going through her desk drawers.

Stomach knotting, she asked, "Can I help you?" far more coolly than she was feeling.

The short man jumped and twisted around, shoving his sandy hair away from his long face. Hank Riddell, Project Cypress research fellow and the man who'd found Artur dead.

"Miss Fanshaw."

"Hank. What exactly are you looking for?"

"A—a folder for Dr. Ulrich."

"That's why you're searching my drawers?"

Hank's spine stiffened and he rocked upward on his toes as if trying to make himself appear more important and said, "He wanted that information that he asked you for on Bio-Chem Tracker!"

Claire swept by him and picked up the folder that sat

on top of the pile. "It's right here, Hank. I don't see how you could have missed it."

He grabbed it from her and quickly backed up. "I'll take it to him." His hands were trembling slightly and his skin had a greenish cast.

"I would have done that first thing this morning as I promised Dr. Ulrich I would, but fine. You certainly can take the information to him." As the research fellow started to leave, she said, "Hank, wait a minute. I want you to realize your actions here were inappropriate."

"I was acting on Dr. Ulrich's orders!" he said, as if that were more important than anything.

To him, perhaps it was. He was a toady with a new Ph.D. A suck-up who would do anything for advancement. Various employees, not only the security guards, had made complaints about the baby scientist. Apparently he thought there should be a pecking order and he was on top of the heap.

"I'm the supervisor of computer services and this is my department, my office. I don't take kindly to your coming into my office and searching my desk, and I don't expect it to happen again. You ask me if you need something and I'll get it for you. Are we clear on that?"

"You weren't here!"

Claire would be surprised that he was arguing with her about this if she hadn't seen him do the same with the security team more than once. Hank Riddell was a self-important little man who thought he was above the rules.

"It's before hours, Hank." Her words were curt but she didn't care. "I'm early. Or maybe you were counting on my not being here for another half hour."

His mouth opened and he gaped at her like a big fish trying to get air. She knew he wanted to argue with her and, for a moment, she thought he might. Then he must have thought better of it, because without saying anything, he spun on his heel and raced out of her office.

Claire stood staring after him, thinking it had been convenient that he'd found the janitor dead in a non-working lab. And wondering what exactly he'd thought to find in her desk.

STAY PUT. RIGHT. Bray threw down the note Claire had left him. Did she really think he was going to wait around, sit on his hands all day till she got home?

And then what?

It wasn't like she'd divulged a plan of action.

Bray microwaved a cup of the lukewarm coffee she'd made not so long ago and raided the tiny refrigerator under the counter for food. The stock was pitiful, but he did come away with a couple of eggs he could scramble. And a look in the cupboards revealed some bread for toast.

Cooking for himself felt natural, like he was used to it. Maybe he was. No matter how hard he tried, he couldn't conjure Claire in a domestic scene. Not even in bed. Well, not before last night.

The blonde, though, was a different story. That dream had popped something in his brain. He remembered them clinking shot glasses together, dancing to some honky-tonk kind of music and then ripping off each other's clothes. Things were still fuzzy after that.

It would come to him, though. Things were starting to come to him unbidden.

As he worked around the kitchen, he got impressions of Claire. Her eating out of take-out cartons and drinking straight from the plastic milk bottle.

He felt her everywhere, especially inside him. It had been that kind of night. Unforgettable. With heat so sizzling between them, how had he forgotten everything personal that had come before?

In his mind's eye, he could see her at Cranesbrook, parked behind her desk, the furrow of her brow a sure indication she was annoyed with him. None of the soft memories he would expect a husband to have of his wife.

A fact that niggled at him all through breakfast and a quick shower and half-assed shave accomplished with a razor that Claire had dulled on her legs. *That* he could see, almost as if he'd been there watching. Only he hadn't. He'd never been on this boat before.

Touching her things fed him memories of her. Moods. Tears. For him? Had she cried herself to sleep every night that he'd been missing?

And then it hit him. He was picking up a lot of her on this boat. She had clothing and all kinds of personal items here, too. She said she'd been keeping an eye on the boat for a friend. She hadn't said she'd been living here. Could there have been some reason she'd had to leave their home? Or was he right not to give her his trust?

He was going to find out.

Had he always had this ability to pick up memories by touching objects? Or was this somehow connected to the "accident" in the lab? Gut instinct rather than memory made him doubt the official story he'd read in the newspaper.

Cleaned up, he felt like a new man. Now if only he could get himself some clean clothes, as well. And a vehicle. Not to mention some cash.

He pulled out the key ring that had miraculously stayed in his pants' pocket. House keys, car keys, other keys that gave him the impression of an office door, one he couldn't quite place. If he could find home, would he find the vehicle, too? With a little luck, he could get inside both.

Now to change his looks a bit so no one would recognize him right off. Hoping it would fit him, he pulled a man's navy windbreaker from the closet. Not his style. He knew that right off. A little snug in the shoulders, it zipped up okay. He put on a billed cap—also not his style—and a pair of wraparound sunglasses he'd found on the kitchen counter. Then he checked himself out in the mirror. The "disguise" would do. He set out for the marina building.

The few customers in the café didn't even give him a second look when he entered.

He approached the counter and a friendly looking middle-aged waitress. "Excuse me, but do you have a pay phone?" When the woman's eyebrows raised in surprise, he explained, "Forgot to charge the cell last night."

"Oh, sure, honey. Over there." She pointed to the opposite side of the café.

"Thanks."

He was in luck. There was even a phonebook. And in it, a listing for Brayden Sloane at Turtle Creek. He copied down his address, then approached the counter again.

"Can you tell me how to get to this address?" he asked, holding out the paper.

"Take the road north about a mile to the second intersection. Then head east and you'll see a road that ends in a T. That's Pine Grove Road. I don't know how far up you have to take it, though."

"Thanks again," he said, slipping her a tip he really couldn't afford.

"Thank you, honey."

Bray left the café, hoping not only to find home and car, but some answers, as well.

EMBROILED IN A STAFF meeting for the better part of the morning, Claire felt like she couldn't wait a moment longer when it finally ended. Before Dr. Ulrich could slip away, she quickly took the opportunity to approach him about his research fellow. Ulrich was on the slender side but tall enough that Claire had to look up at him.

"I hope that information on the program is what you needed," she said.

"What?"

Behind wire-framed glasses, Ulrich's pale blue eyes seemed unfocused. Then again, he'd seemed distracted throughout the meeting, as if he'd had some place he'd rather be. In his lab, no doubt.

"Bio-Chem Tracker, the research program you're interested in buying. Hank Riddell did give you the folder this morning, right?"

"Research program..." He seemed to snap to. "Yes, of course, the computer program. I haven't had time to look at the information yet. I'll let you know if I want to buy sometime next week."

"I thought you needed it immediately since you sent Riddell to get it from my office before work hours."

"I gave no such orders …" He started and blinked down at her. "I have myriad more important things to take care of! I'll get to it when I get to it."

So why did he sound so defensive? Claire wondered, murmuring, "Of course."

And why would he lie about telling Hank…or was it Hank who'd lied?

Still seeming distracted, the director of research hurried off before she could talk to him about the way the folder had been obtained. Claire had reason to wonder anew what the research fellow actually had been looking for in her desk.

The room had cleared and so she stayed behind to share her concerns over Riddell with her boss, Dr. Martin Kelso, acting president of Cranesbrook. Unlike Ulrich, Kelso seemed to be a bundle of focused energy, and his neatly parted dark hair and perfectly creased trousers and pressed shirt reflected his attention to detail.

"Dr. Kelso, do you have a minute?"

"Certainly, Ms. Fanshaw." Kelso's amiable smile made the corners of his dark eyes crinkle. "If it's about your leaving early today, I have no objections. You've been putting in more than your fair share around here."

"No, that's not it." She kept her voice light so her guilt wouldn't show through. "I mean, thank you, but there's something else."

"What is it?"

"Hank Riddell."

"Hank? Is there a problem?"

Uh-oh. He'd used the research fellow's first name. Kelso only did that with employees he really liked.

"Um, I hope there's no problem. But this morning, I found him going through my desk."

"What?"

"If I hadn't come in early, I wouldn't have caught him. When I asked if I could help him, he got all defensive and said he was looking for information on a research program that I had gathered for Dr. Ulrich."

"Perhaps he simply realized the inappropriateness of his actions."

"Maybe. But he made it sound like Dr. Ulrich wanted that folder immediately. I just spoke to Dr. Ulrich and he said he didn't tell Riddell to get the folder."

"You're saying Hank lied?"

Claire shrugged her shoulders and gave Kelso an embarrassed smile. "You know, it's just that so much has been going on here, what with the lab accident and then Mr. Edmonston and a couple of police being murdered...."

Kelso's expression went grim and his forehead pulled tight. "Surely you don't think Hank had anything to do with any of that mess?"

Obviously, Kelso didn't, so Claire backed up mentally as best she could. "I don't think Hank's a murderer or anything. It's just that it all started with that accident in Lab 7. Hank's lab. And now he's acting weird. That's all. I just thought I would bring it to your attention."

Kelso was frowning, rubbing his forehead as though she'd given him a headache.

"Well, thank you, Ms. Fanshaw," Kelso said, his voice cooler than usual. "If that's all…?"

"That's it," she said, inching toward the door. "I'll get back to work now. I'll be here until midafternoon if you need me for anything."

Claire would like to be a fly on the wall when either Kelso or Ulrich had a conversation with Riddell. It seemed the research fellow was acting on his own. She'd thought he'd simply been officious and rude earlier, but now she was beginning to wonder about him.

What *had* he been looking for in her desk? And after stumbling across poor Artur's body…

Assuming it had been a stumble.

What else? Lab 12 was vacant, waiting to be updated. Right?

Claire knew she needed to find out for herself.

In her office, she returned a few phone calls and wished the boat had a phone so she could call Bray to make sure everything was okay.

What was she going to do about him?

Or with him?

She couldn't just make him hang around while she waited for his memory to return. Not that she knew how to force it. And when he did start remembering, he would know she'd lied, so why would he share anything else with her? If she were lucky, perhaps his memory would be selective.

Claire went online to get additional information on the research program Ulrich wanted. Printing it out, she waited until the middle of the noon hour when nearly everyone in the facility would be in the lunchroom.

Less probability of her getting caught. Then she stuffed the new information in a folder—camouflage again in case she actually ran into one of the scientists—and headed for the research wing.

Halfway down the corridor, a woman in a white coat left her laboratory, a cell phone to her ear.

"Tell your brother to come to the phone now…. No, now!" The woman was too embroiled in some domestic problem to do more than give Claire a polite nod as she continued down the hall. "Jimmy, how many times have I told you to listen to Rhonda? Do you want a time-out?"

Claire suspected from the woman's on-edge tone that all the time-outs in the world weren't going to straighten out little Jimmy. She glanced back once to make sure the woman was still distracted as she got to the door of Lab 12. Counting on an empty lab being open, she took a deep breath and tried the handle.

It gave.

The door swung open and she slipped inside, her gaze roaming the room, checking every corner. Not that she expected to find another Bray here, Claire thought, unable to stop thinking about him and their night of little sleep. The room was definitely empty but for lab tables and chairs. And a pail and mop pushed to one side of the storeroom door. Artur's cleaning tools.

She stopped and said a silent prayer in the old man's behalf. She hadn't known him well, but he'd always been friendly to her.

Taking a deep breath, she then caught it. The horrible smell.

Holding her breath for a moment, Claire made for

the storeroom door. She couldn't avoid seeing what looked like bits of partially digested food clinging to the mop. The old janitor must have heaved his cookies before having that heart attack. But what in the world had he been eating?

Claire was glad to escape into the storeroom and close the door behind her. She clicked on the light and saw that this room was still in use. The shelves were loaded with janitorial products, cleaners and paper towels and such.

Disappointed that she'd hit another dead end, she turned to leave when a glint off glass caught her attention. She stepped to the shelving, stooped and moved a carton of degreasers to the side.

Her pulse sped up when she spotted test tubes partially filled with different-colored liquids. What were they doing among the cleaning supplies? she wondered. Could they be left over from when this lab was in operation?

Somehow, she doubted it. What she didn't doubt was that they were dangerous.

Part of her wanted to take the vials and just get out of there, take them somewhere to be tested. What would that prove? She had no idea. Even if the chemicals could be identified, who would know what to do with them?

A bigger problem was getting them out sight unseen. It would be just her luck to run into someone returning from lunch.

Clenching her jaw in frustration, Claire set the box of degreasers back the way she'd found it, and then caught sight of plastic spoons and a black metal contraption next to the chemicals.

She pulled out the device and frowned at what looked like a rectangular box with a bowl-like top. No markings on the body to tell her what it was supposed to be. Was this meant for use with the chemicals? Not just to mix them, which could be done in a beaker, but for some other purpose?

Realizing she was taking too long, Claire replaced the device and made sure to leave everything in its proper place. Maybe if she told Bray about it, he would have some clue as to what it could be used for.

She left the lab just in time. She'd gotten halfway down the corridor when voices alerted her that she was about to come face-to-face with workers coming back from lunch. She recognized one voice in particular—Hank Riddell.

The research fellow started when he saw her. Then his expression darkened.

"Hank, there you are," Claire said breezily, as if she hadn't verbally reamed him out just a few hours before.

"What are you doing in the lab area?" he asked, his gaze shifting to a spot over her shoulder.

He was looking in the direction from which she'd come, but there was no way he could possibly know she'd been in Lab 12.

And if he did figure it out?

What then?

"I found some additional information on Bio-Chem Tracker that didn't make it into the folder you took," she said, holding it out to him. "It's basically testimonials. Might help Dr. Ulrich make that decision about purchasing the program." She simply couldn't help herself. "What did he think of what you brought him?"

Hank stared at her for a moment before saying, "He was favorably impressed. He wanted further time to analyze it, though."

"Of course."

Hank was nearly as good a liar as she, Claire thought. To what purpose, though?

"I need to get to my lab," he muttered, shoving past her.

Claire took a big breath and counted to ten so she wouldn't see red. If ever there was a more rude man, she didn't know who that might be.

Not that she had time to dwell on it. She needed to finish up a few urgent matters still in her in-basket, pull up an HR report on Bray and then get back to the marina before he flew the coop.

Chapter Seven

His thumb simply wasn't working as well as it had the day before.

Bray managed to get one ride and had to walk the rest of the way. Finally he was within yelling distance of the address that had been listed for him at Turtle Creek.

Rather than walk straight down the street, he kept to the perimeter on his approach, using trees and bushes and anything else he could for cover. He half expected to find a team of cops staked out in front of the place, just waiting to bring him in. But as he drew close enough to see a red-brick house with white trim appear among the trees, all looked peaceful. Not a car in sight but the decade-old black Corvette in the drive.

His car. His house.

No one around.

Fishing the keys from his pocket, he loped across the road to the front door. In a flash, he had it unlocked and himself inside.

And then he stopped dead, expecting something…

What?

He looked to his right at the box installed next to the door and realized he was supposed to punch in a security code. A memory…he was getting a memory without touching something. If he didn't disarm the system, an alarm would be set off at the Five Star office and one of the security guards would send the local police over to investigate.

But the alarm wasn't armed.

He did touch the box and heard a female voice saying, *Front door open,* and seeing a delicate hand punch in the code, turning off the system.

A woman…brown hair with blond streaks…a heart-shaped face…gray eyes like his own.

Echo.

So his sister had been here.

Enough sunlight came in through the windows that he didn't have to turn on a light. The living room opened into a dining area, and beyond that a kitchen area. Double-glass doors led to a covered porch over-looking a beautiful view of Turtle Creek.

Bray looked around, hoping to find something familiar, something that would jog his memory.

The place was a little messy with papers strewn on a table and a couple of open drawers in a wall cabinet. He started to shut one of the drawers and he saw a man poking through it. A cop. The cops had been here, but how had they gotten inside? The house hadn't been broken into. No broken window. Front door intact. Someone with a key must have let them in. Echo, no doubt.

Did his own sister believe he was some kind of villain that she'd worked with the authorities against him? The possibility saddened him.

He looked around at the living area, nicely furnished in the basics: a mahogany-colored leather sofa, matching chair and ottoman, a glossy black coffee table and side tables with modern lamps, a distressed-wood dinner table and leather-cushioned wood chairs. There were even a couple of modern brown and dark red area rugs.

A very no-nonsense, masculine decor.

The only personal item softening the living area was a framed photo of a smiling young woman holding a baby. He picked it up and remembered the baby grabbing onto his finger and gurgling at him. Zoe. His niece. He touched her face, a lump in his throat as he wondered if the authorities were any closer to finding her.

If only he had a memory and didn't have the cops on his own back he would find her himself.

And then he looked into Echo's face and remembered him threatening a prepubescent boy who'd given her a hard time. Her introducing him to his first girlfriend. Him rushing her to the hospital when she went into labor. Myriad memories swamped him like a montage in a movie. It came home to him that clearly he and his sister had been each other's support system, especially since he'd come back to civilian life.

The military…

The blonde… He remembered her, too, and the reason he'd been forced to leave the army.

Bray replaced the framed photo, wishing he could see Echo, so he could at least give his sister the support she needed until her child was returned to her. That she might not trust him darkened his mood.

Running his hand over the sofa gave an image of him sprawled out on it, snoozing. The chair gave him an image of him reading the Sunday paper. At the dining table, he remembered eating breakfast.

Alone.

Every impression he got of this place was him alone.

How could that be if Claire was his wife?

He quickly went through the rest of the house. The two-bedroom, office and single bath were all masculine. No bubble baths or shower gels. No feminine clothes or frilly underwear in the closets or drawers. Running his hand over the desk in the office told him where to find a credit card and several hundred dollars in cash. The dock on his desk was empty; touching it, he saw a guy in a dark suit removing the laptop. Probably a Fed.

There were no memories of Claire ever having been anywhere in this house.

He put on clean underwear, tan slacks and a light blue cotton sweater and packed another change of casual clothing in an overnighter.

He picked up no memories of what kind of a man he was, either, a fact that still troubled him.

But his suspicion was confirmed. Claire had lied about being his wife to get him to come with her.

The question was why.

And what was he going to do about it?

DISTRACTED BY THOUGHTS of Bray as she left the Cranesbrook lot, Claire wasn't sure when the low, black car had pulled up behind her. It stayed the same distance behind, even when she put on some speed.

Slowing in the hope that the other car would pass her, Claire felt her pulse speed up when it slowed, too. What was going on here? Was the person behind the wheel following her?

Perhaps her extracurricular activities hadn't gone unnoticed, after all.

Her thoughts went straight to Hank Riddell and her finding him searching her office.

What had he been looking for? If not the folder that had been practically under his nose, then what? And the way he'd stared at her in the hallway…he'd definitely seemed suspicious of her. But if he had reason to be suspicious about something, then he'd had something to hide. Something about the lab accident?

Did Riddell think she knew something she shouldn't?

Could the research fellow be stalking her?

Telling herself not to panic, she stepped on the gas. No matter how many times she checked her rearview mirror, the black car was right there behind her.

The road leading into town and the marina came into view. Now what?

She hesitated at the stop sign for a moment, and suddenly the black car was next to her. Her pulse thundered through her as the tinted window lowered. But when she got a look at the driver, her temper flared.

"What on earth were you thinking following me like that?" she yelled at Bray whose expression remained calm. "Were you trying to cause an accident?"

"Do you have reason to be paranoid?" he asked.

"No, of course not."

"Good. Then follow me into town so you can park. We'll take my car."

"To where?" she asked. "And why not park at the marina?"

No answer. His window was already rolling upward and the Corvette was rolling into the intersection.

So he'd gone home to get his car. Claire guessed she should have known. Brayden Sloane wasn't an undemanding man. When he got focused on something, he wasn't easily deterred. Apparently his loss of memory hadn't changed that trait.

Or was he starting to get his memory back? Was that why he was acting so weird?

Nervous now, Claire followed him into town and parked on a side street, then got into the low-slung Corvette.

"So what's the mystery?" she asked, unable to keep the tightness from her voice. "Where are you taking me?"

"To Baltimore."

"Baltimore?" Baltimore had nothing to do with her. The tightness in her chest eased. "That's at least two hours of driving this time of the afternoon. Whatever for?"

"Because that's where Gage Darnell lives. He must know something about what happened to us. He can fill in some of the blanks in my memory."

"Why do you want to take that chance on him?"

Even though Gage might have some information that would be of use to her, Claire didn't know that. She also didn't know how he would react to seeing Bray. One wild card at a time was enough for her to handle. She was counting on Bray's help to get the information she needed to figure out what had happened to Mac. And

Gage knew she and Bray weren't married. He could ruin everything for her. She'd rather try to handle Bray herself, get at that selective memory she was hoping to jog.

So she asked, "Are you certain your partner will welcome you back with open arms?"

"Gage can fill in the blanks for me. Is there some reason you don't want me to see him?"

"I'm only concerned about *you*. The authorities think you might have been involved in the lab explosion. Gage could turn you in."

"He won't."

"How can you be so sure?"

"When you depend on each other for your lives for three years, that's not an easily broken bond."

"You remember Afghanistan?"

She'd pulled up Bray's HR file and knew that he and Gage had served together in that conflict. She'd dug deeper and found that Bray had left the military before his tour was up. No reason, no hint of dishonor, no medical caveat. Something was up with that, only she didn't know what. The army had needed men. They weren't going to let a seasoned Special Ops sergeant go without good reason.

Which increased her unease at having gotten so close to him. She really didn't know what kind of a man he was. Indeed, he might be dangerous.

"I *am* starting to remember certain things," Bray admitted. "Finally. I imagine all due to you."

She waited for him to say he remembered that he didn't particularly like her and no way would he be married to her. But if he knew, he kept his own counsel.

So maybe he didn't remember now. But if other things were coming back to him, it was only a matter of time before the truth smacked him upside the head. Or a matter of a face-to-face with Gage Darnell.

How long would it be before Bray exposed her lie? And her?

HE WAITED UNTIL DARK to drive to the marina.

Checking over the few vehicles parked there assured him Claire Fanshaw was elsewhere. Good. Better for him. He was still careful as he approached the boat. For all he knew, Sloane could be on board.

"Hello, Claire Fanshaw," he called, as if he were actually hoping to find her. Just in case.

No answer.

He wondered what she would say if he told her he'd brought her a present.

Climbing aboard, he called out again. "Hello, I'm looking for Claire Fanshaw."

Silence. He tried the door. Locked. Damn! Not that he couldn't break it open if he set his mind to it, but he didn't want the woman or the former security chief to know that anyone had been here. He didn't want them to suspect that anything was wrong.

Walking around the boat, looking for another opening, he noticed a porthole had been left open a few inches. He tried to get a look inside, but all was dark until he took out his flashlight. He was staring into the head.

Swinging open the porthole, he dropped the backpack through the opening, then struggled through himself. His gift was cerebral, not physical, so it took some fancy maneuvering, but he managed to get himself inside in one piece.

He exited the head to the galley and shone the flashlight around the room, over a single dish and a mug and a pan in the sink, the only indication that someone had been here recently. Only one person. But when he ventured into the sleeping area he knew he'd been correct.

The woman was indeed hiding the former security chief here.

More than hiding the man, he thought with a grimace as the smell of stale sex assaulted him. He flashed his light over the rumpled sheets, disgusted that she was doing Sloane, too.

All the more reason to take care of them both.

Together.

He slid open the storage drawer beneath the bed and pulled aside some linens. Carefully he set the timer on the device and shoved it to the rear of the drawer, then moved the linens back in place in front of it.

Claire Fanshaw and Brayden Sloane were going to get a big bang out of his little gift.

He could hardly wait until midnight.

Chapter Eight

"So far, all this driving has been for nothing."

Bray thought Claire sounded more relieved than aggravated, no doubt because a face-to-face with Gage would have ended her game, whatever it was. He'd thought to leave a note telling his partner where to find him, but at the last minute had changed his mind. Until he started remembering the lab accident at Cranesbrook in detail, he meant to lie low. He wanted to keep his fate in his own hands.

"We're not done yet," he said. "We might be able to find Gage at Five Star."

Or at least find some information that would help. Or even some object to jog his memory.

"Why don't you just call the office first to see if he's there?"

"I don't want to alert anyone else that I'm coming. Any of the security guards who've been working for us for a while would know my voice. Surprise is the best approach, the reason I didn't try to call Gage at home."

Claire sighed. "No, instead we just spent more hours on the road only to find the house locked up tight."

Bray didn't respond to Claire's grousing. She'd been out of sorts since the interminable traffic backup caused by an accident on the bridge. They'd sat over Chesapeake Bay without moving an inch for more than an hour. And the first thing he'd done when arriving in Annapolis was to take the time to buy a prepaid cell phone before going on to Baltimore. Since it was now past dinnertime, Claire undoubtedly needed to be fed. He could use a decent meal himself. They hadn't had anything to eat since leaving St. Stephens that afternoon, and he didn't know if she'd actually had lunch.

Though he'd like to confront Claire about her lies, Bray decided to bide his time with her, as well. He would see how long it would take her to be truthful with him, if ever. He hated lies. He'd remembered that the moment he'd placed the blonde from his dream the night before.

Part of him regretted Claire really wasn't his wife, considering the heat they'd generated most of the night. Every time he so much as looked at her, he had an erection. If he touched her, he might lose it and fall into that trap again. So how was he going to avoid sharing a bed later?

Claire broke into his thoughts, asking, "Do you actually have a clue about the Five Star operation?"

"I know a couple of guards work around the clock keeping tabs on monitors and alarms." It seemed using his mind to think his way through his situation was making his memory less selective.

"How are we going to get past them?"

"There's a rear entrance near the Dumpster." After having touched the mystery keys on his key ring enough, he had a vague picture of the setup. "I seem to remember a hallway leading to the conference room and private offices. I don't even know if I still have an office here since getting the contract with Cranesbrook. I obviously moved to St. Stephens to run the operation, so how often would I have reason to drive all the way into Baltimore?"

"So your memory is coming back," Claire said.

"Some." He thought she sounded worried. Good. That would teach her to lie. "Then again, if anyone would know how often I was gone, it would be you, right? I mean, who would know better than my wife?"

"As I said, we haven't been together very long."

"How long?"

Tension tightened her voice when she said, "A few weeks before the accident."

"So we're newlyweds."

"Yes."

"That would explain why your stuff isn't all over the house."

Bray sensed Claire was frozen to the passenger seat waiting for the other shoe to drop. In thinking about why she would have fabricated this life together, he'd figured she must have good reason for the pretense, the main reason he hadn't ended the charade.

If only he knew her motivation…

He decided to go on as if he hadn't figured out she was gaming him.

"The visit to the house was productive. I put some things together by going through the place, especially my home office."

He didn't admit how he'd regained some memories—

that touching objects had given him knowledge. As far as he could tell, the bizarre ability was a recent acquisition, and it didn't take a genius to relate it back to the accident at Cranesbrook Associates.

What the hell had they been testing in Lab 7?

Did Claire know? Was that why she'd shown up in the lab the night before? What if she'd pretended to be his wife simply to keep him quiet?

She could be working for the authorities.

Or the competition.

He wanted in the worst way to believe her motivation was altruistic.

On the way to Cranesbrook, he'd stopped for coffee and hadn't been able to resist getting on one of the café's computers. He'd taken the time to run a security check on Claire. If she had anything to hide, he hadn't been able to find what that might be.

What reason would she have to go so far in her deception as to sleep with him? Unless her attraction to him had simply outweighed her good sense. Remembering the sex they'd shared, he deemed it hot enough to set the boat on fire. He was getting hot now, just thinking about it. Maybe their chemistry was too combustible to ignore.

Even so, he tried his best.

The Five Star offices were located in a strip mall. The security business was snugged between a vet's office and a day spa, all closed to customers for the night. Bray drove around the back and pulled the car between two Dumpsters and two doors set near the center of the building. Either door could be the security office entrance.

"Are you sure this is a good idea?" Claire asked as they got out of the Corvette.

"It's the only one I have that might jog some memories about Cranesbrook for me. How about you?"

Bray stared at her for a moment, until she shrugged and looked away. Then he removed the key ring from his pocket, he'd figured out the keys that didn't belong to the car or the house must belong to the offices here. When he'd touched them earlier, he'd had the image of a bank of monitors and he'd remembered the basic office setup. He simply picked one of the doors, but when he touched the handle and got an impression of a woman with four dogs on leashes, he knew this wasn't the correct choice.

He automatically moved to door number two on the other side of the Dumpster.

"You didn't even try your keys," Claire said. "How do you know the first door isn't the right one?"

"Instinct," he responded, unwilling to share more with someone he didn't exactly trust.

One touch of the second doorknob and he knew this was the right entrance. Putting a finger to his lips to keep Claire quiet, he unlocked the door and opened it a crack while listening intently for any sounds in the hallway. When he heard none, he opened the door a bit wider and peered into the dimly lit interior to make sure no one was there. All clear. He signaled Claire and led the way inside.

Somehow Bray knew the offices and conference room were on the left side of the hall, but he didn't know which door led to which room. The first one opened to the conference room. The second to an office so neat he knew it had to be in disuse. His, then. They had to pass the windowed door to the main office. He stopped and carefully peered inside so as not to be seen. Two uniformed security guards sat at their stations, one of them on the phone, the other adjusting a monitor.

He sensed neither of the men was Gage. Damn! He could use his partner now. They'd always watched each other's backs.

Another memory suddenly zapped him. One from Afghanistan. The source of his nightmares.

His head began to throb and burn.

Before he could tumble over that edge, he shoved away the past and continued on to the front office, Claire so close behind him, he could practically feel her against his back. He turned to face her and she brushed up against his chest. Her eyes widened and the breath caught in her throat, making a funny little noise that zapped him with renewed lust. For a moment he gave in to the personal heat, imagined taking her in his arms and kissing her right there.

Muffled laughter coming at them through the wall cut through the moment. The security guards must be sharing a joke. He frowned, hoping that didn't mean they were shirking their responsibilities.

Pushing Claire into his partner's office, Bray followed, closing the door before turning on the light. They were alone. He wanted her again. He had to stop this, had to learn to control the raw attraction he felt toward her.

"Your partner isn't here," she said, not quite meeting his gaze.

Bray steeled himself against the memories of her—fresh, raw and undeniable. "But his computer is."

The CPU was silent but a glowing light told him it was set to hibernate. Bray turned on the monitor, tapped the mouse and a screen came up demanding a password.

"Do you know his password?" Claire asked, crowding him.

Did she have to stand so close? Was she doing so on purpose to distract him? Bray wouldn't put it past her. But distract him from what?

He touched the keyboard and concentrated on the screen and password request. It was as if he could see Gage two-fingering it in.

"Got it."

"How?"

Ignoring Claire, Bray typed s-c-i-e-n-c-e-g-e-e-k. Seconds later, he was in.

"Bray, how did you figure that out?"

"I'm psychic."

"No, really?"

"Gage is my partner."

"So he gave you his password? When? You haven't even spoken to him since the accident."

Not answering, Bray quickly acquainted himself with Gage's setup. When he found the Cranesbrook folder, he called it up. These were shared files, so it would stand to reason that most of what was here was information he'd entered. He would have looked at these files at home…if his computer had been there.

"What are you looking for?"

"I'll know it when I see it."

Bray opened the view to get details, then went through one subfolder at a time. He was looking for any file that had an entry dated after the accident.

There was only one, dated a few days before. He opened it and Claire leaned over his shoulder, giving him a whiff of a scent that was at once subtle and sensual.

"What did you find?" she murmured, her warm breath stirring the flesh around his ear.

"Looks like Gage made some notes about the accident."

And staring at them, Bray realized the listing seemed familiar somehow. Concentrating, he remembered his partner sometimes used shorthand messages to himself when he was trying to figure things out. The memories kept coming. He could hear Gage telling him that putting his thoughts in writing stimulated his right brain, which led to some creative solutions, especially when working on one of his electronic inventions.

Gage was a gadget junky. Bray remembered this clearly. Trying not to get too excited, he concentrated on the notes in front of him on the LCD monitor.

—alarm goes off and brings Bray and me running to Lab 7

—smoke fills the area, Vanderhoven out on floor, then some kind of explosion knocks me out

—I wake up at Beech Grove loony bin, Vanderhoven likewise, Bray missing

—Riddell sneaking around—to see Vanderhoven? co-workers/friends from Cranesbrook

—held prisoner but find I have a new gift

—I escape by using my mind to open doors and take Lily on the run

By "using my mind," did he mean telekinesis? Combine that power with his own ability to see the past by touching things, and something really weird was going on.

Hoping to learn more about what had happened to them, Bray continued reading.

—Beech Grove janitor dead, Detective Rand McClellan after me
—Riddell confined to Cranesbrook, doesn't leave
—Detective Richard Francis killed
—Edmonston definitely guilty—Lily gets him on tape—but did he have help? Bray?
—Bray guilty? if not, where? injured? dead?
—police officer killed at Cranesbrook
—Edmonston dead, but body count mounting—why? who else has investment in experiment?
—Kelso and Morton seen together having dinner
—McClellan asks strange questions about Vanderhoven—can the lab assistant open doors with his mind, too?
—Zoe taken and Bray is the ransom

"Ransom!" Bray exclaimed. "What the hell?"

"You're the ransom? I don't understand. Why would the villain who took Zoe do so to get to you?"

"Maybe I know too much."

Maybe he was guilty.

He read the last entry.

—I raid Cranesbrook files again looking for connections outside the institute—one of Riddell's employment references is Dr. Martin Kelso

"Riddell and Kelso—that makes sense," Claire said. "Dr. Kelso only calls certain employees by their first names. Hank Riddell is one of them. What are you thinking?" she asked as he printed out the list.

"That I have to turn myself in."

"Would that be wise?"

"My niece is missing, Claire." He shut down the file, then put the computer back into hibernate. "I would give myself directly to the bastard who has her, but I don't know how to do that. The authorities do."

Claire didn't say anything as he returned the room to the way he found it, but he could feel her tension.

He pressed an ear to the door to make sure he couldn't hear anyone on the other side. Then he grasped the handle and was frozen by a vision of two men. His memory kicked in, making him certain the muscular, seasoned-looking guy with the military haircut was Gage. The other man—a natty dresser—he didn't recognize.

"I know I agreed to stick around Baltimore in case you need me, Detective McClellan, but…"

"You planning to take a trip?"

"Just over the state line in Delaware. Rehoboth Beach. A place called the Sunrise Bed and Breakfast."

"Sounds nice."

Gage shrugs. "I'll bring my laptop. I promised Lily we'd spend some uninterrupted time together. And I need to know she's safe."

"Not a bad idea. With some of the strange things going on around here…"

Gage can't hide his surprise. "More strange things?"

The stranger shakes his head. "You don't want to know."

Chapter Nine

"Bray, are you all right?"

Jarred back to the present by Claire, Bray frowned down at her and thought *he* certainly wanted to know what kind of strange things the cop meant. Odd that he'd had more than the quick images he normally got. The scene had played out as if he'd seen it in live action. He tried the door handle again, but this time it gave him zero.

"Fine. I'm fine."

He led the way out to the Dumpster area and his car, wondering what other strange things were going on. Gage was able to open doors with his mind. He himself was able to pick up on other people's memories by touching objects.

What could Wes Vanderhoven do with *his* mind? Bray wondered, remembering the dreams.

Vanderhoven must have been the guy out cold on the floor. Whatever breathing in those chemicals had done to him and Gage, they had done to the lab technician, too.

Once in the car, Claire said, "Turning yourself in could be the biggest mistake you ever make."

"A baby is at risk—my niece. I can't let anything happen to her because of me. I couldn't live with that."

"Let's go directly to your sister, then. Or we can call Echo…"

"I tried that last night. The cops are glued to her side. One of them will answer."

"I know that. But I'll do the calling and ask for her, get her to talk to me. It's worth a try."

Claire must really be desperate not to let him get away from her. But he had to admit she had a point. If he went to a police station, they would just keep him locked up until maybe it was too late.

"All right. Try," he said, driving toward the highway that headed south.

Claire got out her cell phone and made the call without contacting directory assistance, leaving Bray wondering how she knew Echo's number in the first place.

"She's not answering." Claire's voice was filled with frustration. "Why wouldn't someone whose kid was missing answer?"

"Maybe she's not there. Call the police, then. Ask to speak to whoever is in charge of the kidnapping case."

"We have some time," she said. "At least an hour and a half before we're in the vicinity. I can try your sister again before putting your fate into the hands of the authorities."

Before losing him and whatever she hoped to get out of him. Bray hated not knowing Claire's motives, but he didn't argue. He wasn't anxious to be locked up, either. Besides, he didn't mind spending more time in the redhead's company.

Claire reached for the radio and turned it on. "Some music will ease the tension."

If only. "Getting my memory back will go a longer way to make me feel better."

True for him. But for Claire, the game would be over. He could call it now if he chose, tell her he knew the truth about their so-called marriage. He didn't know why he didn't put an end to her charade. Maybe because he sensed that, despite her lies, she wasn't a bad person. She must have some powerful reason for hooking up with him.

He would wait and see a bit longer.

"You are still getting some memories, though, right?" she suddenly asked. "When you touched the door handle in Gage's office, what exactly did you remember?"

Realizing she meant just a normal memory, not one of the chemically enhanced ones, Bray was saved from answering by a news bulletin cutting into the music.

"This just in. The Amber Alert for missing child Zoe Sloane is off," a newscaster said. "The baby was returned to her mother, Echo Sloane, a few minutes ago. The police are not yet releasing details, but we do know that Wes Vanderhoven, an employee of Cranesbrook Associates who was involved in that lab accident two weeks ago, had the Sloane baby. Vanderhoven was killed during the rescue. More details as we get them."

"Thank God, Zoe is safe," Bray said, then felt Claire's hand trembling on his thigh as though she were trying to share in his relief.

Glancing at her, Bray swore that despite the dark, he saw Claire's eyes glitter as if they'd filled with tears.

She cared about the outcome of the kidnapping. He could see that for himself. So she couldn't be a terrible person. As he thought about Zoe, his throat grew tight for a moment, but he quickly got back under control.

"Crisis avoided," she murmured.

No doubt Claire assumed she had more time to get whatever it was she wanted out of him. Given the change in circumstances, Bray felt generous and decided to give it to her.

"I don't know about you," he said, "but my legs are feeling pretty hollow."

"Food would be good."

"Annapolis or truck stop?"

"I don't need fancy. Fast would be best."

"Then truck stop it is."

He got off at the next exit and drove straight for the gas station/minimart/café. The lot was crowded with eighteen-wheelers and the café was equally loaded with truckers, but they found an empty booth and a waitress was right on them. After ordering the meat loaf special, Bray sat back and stared at Claire, wondering once again what her deal was.

"Maybe we should look over that list you printed out," she said.

"Think it'll do some good?"

"Why else did you want it?"

Pulling the list from his jacket pocket, he unfolded it and smoothed it out before handing it over to her. He watched her face carefully as she skimmed Gage's notes. Her expression told him she wanted to say something but that she was holding back.

"What?"

"Gage didn't go far enough back in time."

"What do you mean? He started with the lab accident."

"Before that. He missed something."

"Like what?"

Her green eyes were glued to his face when she said, "A lab technician named Mac Ellroy."

"Mac…" He frowned.

"Do you remember him?"

"The name is familiar, but I can't place him."

"He used to work in Lab 7."

Mac Ellroy. Was this guy the reason she was sticking to him like glue? Why? What was her connection to the former Cranesbrook lab tech?

"Odd that Gage didn't mention him in his notes," Bray muttered. "But wait, you said 'before the lab accident.' I don't get it."

"Mac disappeared before the lab accident."

"Disappeared? That sounds ominous."

"The party line is that he left for a better job."

"So why don't you buy it?"

"Things just didn't jibe. And then his HR records disappeared. It's as if he never worked for Cranesbrook Associates."

Bray was certain she'd skipped some critical information there, but he played along. "You looked for his HR records after he left?"

"Yes," she said without explanation. "Trust me, if they were there, I would have found them."

"Why?"

"Because I wanted to find the man, of course."

"Why?" he repeated.

Claire suddenly seemed incapable of giving him an answer, straight or otherwise. A sneaking suspicion that this hunt for the lab tech was personal niggled at him. Surely she and this Mac Ellroy weren't lovers…not when she'd pretended to be *his* wife in every way. Then again, she'd gone pretty far to get what she wanted. Claire chewed on her bottom lip, and Bray steeled himself against her seeming vulnerability and reminded himself that he couldn't necessarily trust anything she said or did.

Recovering, she said, "I thought he might have some critical information. Something to clear *you*."

Her gaze was steady, her body relaxed, her hands quiet on the printout.

Too steady…too relaxed…too quiet.

Claire was lying again.

Bray's stomach tightened and his pulse picked up and strengthened until he could hear its rush through his head. He didn't need a specific memory to know how much he hated lies. His physical reaction was proof enough. He'd thought he could play Claire's game until she finally gave it up, but now he wasn't so sure. Part of him wanted to confront her, to make her spill everything she knew or suspected.

But when that happened, what if she took off? She was his only link to his past, as tenuous as that might be, and he didn't want to be without her.

Thankfully their food arrived, delaying any showdown. Though she had to be as starving as he, Claire picked at her food. Because she'd brought up Mac Ellroy and now was upset thinking about the man? What kind of a personal relationship had she had with him? Had she loved him?

Ignoring the twinge the thought gave him, Bray concentrated on eating.

The rest could wait until they were alone.

CLAIRE HAD ALMOST BROKEN down and told Bray the truth. Everything. Instead he'd gotten a half-truth about her "second-hand" knowledge of Mac's disappearance and good reason to be suspicious of her.

Not that he'd expressed the questions that she'd watched him swallow along with his food. While he'd wolfed down that meat loaf like it was his last meal, the few bites she'd gotten down sat like a lump in her stomach.

Bray's questions would have to be answered sometime. Only not right this moment, which was the reason she pretended to be asleep all the way to St. Stephens.

"Are you out for the night or can you drive?" Bray asked, finally breaking the silence.

She opened her eyes and saw they were at the edge of town. "The Corvette?"

"Your Honda. It's just ahead."

She shifted in her seat and stretched the best she could. "Sure, I'll move it to the marina lot." That would give her a little extra time to get herself together.

Pulling up next to her vehicle, he said, "When we get to the boat, we need to talk."

"Right," she mumbled, opening the door and plunging into the chilly autumn night.

She felt his pale gaze on her all the way to the driver's door. Getting inside was a relief. But her respite was short-lived, ending the moment she parked next to him at the marina. Tension wired her but exhaustion threatened to shut her down. She glanced at the clock—a few minutes to midnight—and wondered if she could put off that talk until morning.

Walking with Bray toward the pier made her feel like she was about to go in front of a firing squad. She was too tired to come up with some story to appease him. If he asked her for the truth, she had nothing else left to give him. And then he would probably walk—no, run—in the other direction.

Why did she care so much what he thought of her?

Because she didn't want him to run from her. She needed an ally.

To be really honest, she needed Bray.

A scary, scary thought. She'd never needed anyone. Not in that way. She'd always depended on herself. Trusting someone else was not part of her makeup. Except for Mac. He'd been there for her when she'd needed rescuing, which was the reason she so desperately wanted to rescue him back, even when she feared it was likely too late.

Bray put an arm around her waist for support as they stepped onto the pier. Claire tried not to tremble, but life as she'd created it for them was about to fall apart. As they drew closer to *Lainie's Moor,* she wished with all her heart there was some way to put off the inevitable.

Her wish was granted as the pier under her feet began to rumble and an ear-splitting explosion blew her world to bits.

Chapter Ten

Bray threw Claire to the pier and covered her with his body as a million shards rained down on them. What was left of the boat was wreathed in smoke and flame.

"What the hell happened?" Claire gasped, but Bray wasn't answering. She shoved at him, made him move off her until she could see his frozen expression and glassy-eyed stare. "Hey, Bray, we're okay." She was terrified, perhaps, and maybe a bit bruised, but she was in one piece.

"We need to get out of here before the enemy returns!" he said in a loud whisper.

She barely heard him over the roar of the pulse rushing through her head.

They needed to get out of there before the authorities arrived or they would be detained for questioning, that was for certain. Should that happen, Bray would be taken in and she would be exposed and would never have another chance to find out what happened to Mac. Not to mention what might happen to Bray if he were caught before they got to the truth. As she scrambled to her feet, her mouth went dry and her heart beat so hard she feared it would burst from her chest.

"Okay, let's go then," she said, fumbling for her cell, knowing that they had to flee. "I can call in the explosion on the move. I hope the fire department gets here fast before the flames spread to one of the other boats."

Claire barely flipped open the phone when Bray wrapped an arm around her back. He kept her crouched over and pushed her back toward the parking lot.

"Not safe!" he barked. "Take cover!"

Indeed, they were out in the open, but what he was saying didn't make sense to her.

Something was wrong with Bray. He was too stiff, too paranoid, his gaze roaming and never stopping, as if he really did expect someone to jump out at them. They were almost to the vehicles when she heard distant sirens coming closer and realized that someone else had already made the call. Or maybe the explosion had shaken the whole town awake. Taking a deep breath, she slipped the cell phone back into her pocket and went for her car keys. The way Bray was acting, she wasn't about to let him drive anywhere.

"We'll take my CRV." It was less distinctive than a Corvette, she thought, and they might need the four-wheel drive where they were going.

He didn't argue. She pushed him toward the passenger side and got in behind the wheel. As he climbed in, she started the engine and sped out of the lot toward a back exit. Flashing red and blue lights lit the marina entrance. White cars like surreal ghosts zoomed into the parking lot from the opposite end. The St. Stephens' police had arrived, followed by the fire department's only truck.

Oh, Lord, she was going to have to tell the Moores…what? How was she going to explain their boat had blown up while in her possession? Were they even insured for a disaster like this? If it took her forever to make the money, Claire vowed she would repay every penny necessary to replace the boat.

Once off the marina grounds, Claire kept going, driving down a narrow road and into a stand of trees that provided cover. Only then did she take the time to stop and look back. The fire already seemed diminished, but from a distance, she couldn't tell what was going on.

That she didn't see any vehicle lights cutting across the parking lot in their direction was a big relief. No one was after them. At least, not for the moment.

"We're clear," she said, but Bray didn't respond. He sat stiffly in his seat and when she touched him, his flesh under her hand was cold. "We're okay, Bray. Everything's okay now."

"The enemy—"

"There is no enemy. Just you and me."

His features remained hardened when he asked, "Did you set a charge to blow up the boat?"

"No, of course not."

Claire blinked. She'd reacted too fast to think about why *Lainie's Moor* had gone up like a fireball. All she'd been worried about was Bray getting out of there before he was discovered. She hadn't stopped to think about why or how the boat had blown up.

But if it had been done deliberately…

"Someone wants me dead," she gasped.

"Who?"

"I—I don't know."

Someone who knew she was snooping into things that were none of her business?

"Someone who knows you're hiding me." Bray's tone was grim. "I knew I shouldn't have gone with you yesterday. Now we're both targets."

Bray was looking out the windows as if he expected the perpetrator to jump out at them any moment. A jittery Claire put the car in gear and drove down a series of back roads and didn't stop until they came to a dead end. They were in an unpopulated area. Even so, she took them off-road and into a rocky tree-sheltered area half surrounded by thick bushes. No one would find them back here, not tonight.

Assuming that anyone was looking for them in the first place. No doubt the villain assumed he'd succeeded in killing them both.

The morning news would clear up that little detail.

Now what? At least Bray seemed to have calmed down a notch or two.

"We can sleep in here tonight," she said, opening her door and setting her feet on the ground.

As she stood, her head went a little woozy, making her pause before getting her bearings and opening up the rear door. Still sitting in the passenger seat, Bray had gone silent on her again. Claire didn't know what to do, what to think. She couldn't focus. She guessed that must be the way Bray was feeling at times.

"The back seat goes down," she told him, trying to sound natural, "and I always keep a blanket and water and other stuff with me, just in case."

Bray finally stirred and let himself out of the vehicle to open the other door. He helped her lower the rear seat back. What he wasn't doing was looking at her.

Claire wanted in the worst way to demand Bray talk to her, tell her what was happening to him. Waiting in silence was one of the hardest things she'd ever done, but sensing he needed time to get himself together, wait she did. She set her laptop and gym bag in the front seat and they climbed into their makeshift bed and locked themselves in for the night. Not that she was going to sleep any time soon. She was way too wired and figured Bray felt the same.

They sat up with their backs against opposite sides of the CRV, the blanket spread out between them and covering their legs, a battery-powered lantern giving them just enough light to see each other.

When she couldn't stand the silence any longer, Claire asked, "Bray, can we talk about your reaction to what happened on the pier?"

"There's nothing to talk about."

"Of course there is. You scared me almost as much as the explosion did."

"I wasn't trying to hurt you."

"I didn't think you were. I was scared for you. *You're* the one who's hurt."

Maybe he had been for a very long time. Claire remembered him tearing up the bed the night before in the throes of a nightmare. His broken muttering had sounded like he was trying to give orders. Military orders.

"You even have bad dreams about whatever it is that happened to you," she continued softly. When he still didn't respond, she took a stab in the dark. "You've never gotten over Afghanistan, have you?"

"How do you know about Afghanistan?"

He was looking at her now, his narrowed gaze pinning her so she couldn't squirm out of answering. She was tempted to let him think he'd told her before and he'd simply forgotten, but she couldn't do that to him. She shouldn't have done any of this to him.

"I looked into your HR records."

That snapped Bray to. "HR has records on me? I'm not a Cranesbrook employee."

"Surely you know the company did full security clearances on you and Gage." Then she realized the irony of her assumption. "Well, if you had your memory back, you would remember."

He would remember a lot of things, including his combative and anything-but-personal relationship with her.

"Afghanistan," he muttered. "I remember…not everything but enough…"

His voice faltered on the last. She couldn't help herself. "Tell me."

For a moment she didn't think he would.

But then he said, "It was a living nightmare. The heat. The bombings. The deaths. We were in hell and couldn't get out." He ran his fingers through his hair and left it in dark spikes. "I don't remember his name…but one of the men in my unit stepped on a land mine right in front of me. They call it pink mist." He paused for a few seconds, then, in a strangled voice, added, "I had to shower for an hour to get him off me."

Claire shuddered. "That must have been awful."

"He exploded just like the boat did tonight. A man I lived with, and ate and fought beside, blew up in front of me and I don't remember his name. What the hell kind of person does that make me?"

His voice was thick with self-recrimination. Claire wanted to cry for the waste of human life he'd seen. She wanted to cry for what Bray must have gone through personally. Survivor guilt could be a bitch.

"It makes you human, Bray. The guy's death still tortures you years after it happened. You might have lost your memory temporarily, but you haven't lost *him* even if you can't recall his name right this moment."

She wondered if the incident had been the spring-board for Bray being released early from his tour of duty. If he'd had some psychological problem, some kind of Post Traumatic Stress Disorder, surely that would have been indicated in his records. Then again, if it had, it would have prevented him from getting the clearance he'd needed to protect government-funded experiments.

What she knew about PTSD might not be extensive, but she remembered that it didn't always show up right away. A person could be doing fine for a long time and then some trigger would set that person off.

Like a lab explosion.

Was that it? Had Bray been ripe for some kind of breakdown? Had the Cranesbrook accident set him off into a major PTSD episode?

"That would explain the memory loss," she murmured.

"What?"

"The lab accident. It wasn't a land mine, but it was another explosion. The noise…the light…"

"If only it was that simple."

"Tell me," she said again.

Only this time he didn't. He sank into a stubborn silence. Instinct made Claire get closer. She crawled to his side of the vehicle and hunkered down next to him.

"I'm on your side."

She meant it. She might be using Bray to get some kind of justice for Mac and closure for herself, but she wanted to clear him, too. Her difficult youth had given her the tools to read people, a kind of self-defense mechanism. She now was certain of what she'd hoped to be true all along—that Bray was a victim, not a villain.

Worse, Claire feared her lies may have signed Bray's death warrant. They'd led him straight to his would-be executioner. Only by luck had they come back to the pier late enough to avoid being blown up.

The only way out of this was to determine who was after them and to get the bastard before he got them.

Knowledge that might be locked in the recesses of Bray's mind.

Her thoughts went back to Gage's notes. He said he'd used his mind to open doors to escape, and wondered if Vanderhoven could do the same.

What could Bray do?

The words tumbled out of her mouth before she could think about them.

"Can you do things with your mind that you couldn't do before the lab accident?"

Though he didn't say anything, Bray's body language gave him away. He drew tight into himself and she knew she'd hit on something. Finally. This was her chance to get him to talk.

"What Gage mentioned in his notes…" Claire said. "Did the accident affect you in the same way?"

"No…I don't think so."

What he didn't say was that it hadn't affected him at all. Which in her mind meant it had.

Pushing, she asked, "What did it do to you, then?" She felt his silent gaze on her. "Bray, please. We want the same thing—to figure out what happened."

He breathed out audibly and nodded. "I get memories…when I touch things."

"Objects help you get your memory back?"

"Not always mine."

Claire started. "I don't understand."

"Join the club."

She waited for Bray to explain, certain that if she pushed too hard, she would hit a wall.

He finally said, "I would touch things…people…and see…visions, I guess you'd call them. A guy wandering drunk along the waterfront, a woman on a playground with kids, an old man getting mugged. At first it was terrifying, like walking through a world of ghosts…none of it real. I thought I was losing my mind. Eventually, I put it together and figured out that what I was doing was picking up memories of other people like some kind of human antenna. That's how I got into Cranesbrook yesterday."

"Let me get this straight. You say you can call up other people's memories at will."

"No, not at will. I just figured out how to use what came to me."

"But you can't call up your own."

Claire hoped Bray might elaborate on that point, but

he didn't. He'd admitted his memory was returning in bits, but could he really force it through touching objects? Through touching *her?*

Should she believe him about any of this? He'd been through a lot. He wasn't himself. War did terrible things to a soldier. As would some chemical cocktail unleashed on an unsuspecting subject.

So did she believe Bray or not? That was the tough question. Not the most pragmatic person, even she had grave doubts about so-called woo-woo stuff. And this "power" he claimed was Woo-Woo with two capital Ws.

"So it sounds crazy, huh?" he finally asked. "*I* sound crazy."

Claire couldn't help herself from testing him. "Get any memories off that blanket?"

He touched the material covering his legs. His forehead pulled into a frown. It took him a minute but then he said, "A picnic. Food spread around you. You're lying on the blanket near the water."

Could be a good guess.

"What about this?" she asked, handing him the battery-run lantern.

This time, his response came slower.

"Flat tire… It's dark and you're on a deserted road…. It flashes a red warning light…. You change the tire yourself."

Claire started but was too surprised at the accuracy of the memory to say anything.

Bray groaned. "Maybe I am crazy. Maybe I'm guilty of whatever they think I did, too."

"You're not crazy."

How could he have known about her roadside emergency? The lab accident had done something to his brain, had given him a power that a normal person didn't have. Going with her instincts, Claire found herself moving closer to Bray and was glad to feel his arm wrap around her.

"And you're not a criminal," she assured him.

"Then what am I?"

"A victim. Of the war. Of Project Cypress."

"So you think the lab accident somehow changed my brain chemistry?"

"Maybe. Gage, too. Vanderhoven, for all we know. And it seems to me that someone at Cranesbrook knows it. Several someones." Since she'd decided Bray wasn't one of the bad guys, Claire needed to share everything she knew for sure. "Maybe that's why Sid Edmonston ran down Evan Buckley. He was one of the security guards working for you and Gage. Evan must have known what was going on."

"And now Edmonston is dead."

"Right," Claire agreed. "Rand McClellan shot him in the line of duty. He's a detective who got involved with the case. Actually, he was helping your sister find Zoe. Sid killed Rand's partner. And then a local cop was killed right in the Cranesbrook offices."

"A lot of deaths connected with that lab accident."

Wishing some of this would jog Bray's memory, Claire nodded. "Your partner was lucky to get out of Beech Grove Clinic alive. A lot of money changed hands there—Cranesbrook straight to Dr. Morton."

"Cover-up money."

"That's not all. The Project Cypress deadline was

moved up. Millions ride on Cranesbrook Associates meeting that new completion date. The researchers, Kelso, Ulrich, Riddell—they're all guilty of trying to cover up the accident of the decade so they can turn over their product and collect their rewards. As far as I can see, you stand between them and that big bonus. Some kind of mistake was made in Lab 7 and you're the living proof."

He looked down into her face. "Me and Gage."

"Yeah, but it seems your partner had the good sense to go underground until this mess is resolved. Unless you can 'remember' where he is, we're on our own."

Bray didn't respond to that, but he shifted against her as he asked, "Any ideas about what we do next?"

Claire shook her head and nestled it against Bray's chest where she could hear his heartbeat quicken. "I don't know, Bray. I wasn't ready for what happened tonight. At the moment, I'm all out of ideas."

But Bray had ideas.

He pulled her closer to him, smoothed the hair from the side of her face and lifted her chin. His expression softened as he looked down at her, and Claire felt her heart beat in an odd rhythm. Something inside her twisted, gave way. Some guard that she'd put up years—no, decades—ago, when people she'd cared about had disappointed her over and over. She'd protected herself against that kind of pain for longer than she could remember.

Until now.

Suddenly she felt stripped of her emotional defenses, vulnerable. She didn't know that she liked it. But she liked Bray.

More than liked him.

Unwilling to put words to what she was feeling, she allowed herself to be distracted by his mouth, which was leaving a soft, wet trail down her forehead and down her cheek, only to stop at her parted lips.

She couldn't help herself. Despite all her resolve to not let this happen again, Claire felt herself melt the moment they connected. She slipped her hands up around his neck and kissed Bray until she was breathless.

Her heart fluttered in her chest, the response elemental and yet something beyond the physical. She wanted—no, needed—to connect with him to assuage the longings she never allowed herself. She wanted him to know that he was different, special, but she couldn't tell him that, not with her lies standing between them. So she showed him, with her lips and her hands and her breasts that she pressed against his chest, how much she needed him.

As though he were protesting, Bray moaned into her mouth and thrust her back until they were horizontal. The vehicle demanded intimacy, and with his hands stroking her into gooseflesh through her clothing, Claire felt closer to him than to any man in her past. Maybe it came from him being so open and honest with her.

If only she could be equally open and honest with him.

No man really knew her. Mac knew her, but as a best friend. He'd been there to see her through some of her darkest moments, inspiring a loyalty that had become her justification for tricking a man already wounded by life.

"Bray," she murmured, wanting to tell him, wanting him to know who she really was before she hurt him, too. "I need you...want you more than anything."

He made a shushing sound and covered her protest with a deep, soul-searing kiss.

Claire let go then and gave herself over. Bray quickly undressed them both with her fumbling assistance.

She didn't know how much longer she had with him, but she would take every moment she could get until he learned the truth and turned away from her for her lies.

There was nothing for it. The damage was already done.

Tucking away the hazy future, Claire allowed herself the present. She spread her thighs and took Bray in and wrapped her legs around his back.

This was all that mattered, she told herself, rocking her hips under him. Someone to cling to for now. She would take what she could get and be satisfied.

Only afterward, after they came together and he collapsed on her, did she realize she'd done the unforgivable.

She'd lied to herself.

The realization kept her from sleeping deeply. And so when Bray became restless and vocal, she was awake to hold him against the heartbreak of his nightmare.

"Claire," he murmured, possessively taking hold of her, trapping her against his body before falling back to sleep.

Claire wondered what she'd been thinking, getting so emotionally wrapped up in a man she hardly knew. She wasn't ready for this. Wasn't ready to be on the run with a fugitive who wasn't really her husband. Not ready to be the focus of an attack. Of someone wanting her dead.

She was caught.

A liar.

She'd fallen into her own trap.

Chapter Eleven

They sent the divers into the water just after dawn.

On scene for the better part of an hour, Detective Rand McClellan leaned back against his car and watched the activity on the pier. Would they bring up a body? Or two?

Pieces, he corrected himself. Pieces of a body or bodies. All depended on how close they had been to the explosion.

Everyone had turned out to see what they would find. In addition to the state fire marshal handling the actual investigation of the explosion, the area was crawling with cops. The locals had come in first, and even though they'd had to hand over the case to the state, they'd stuck around, keeping to themselves. Locals in blue uniforms clustered on one side of the pier, state troopers in tan and brown on the other, a couple of Feds in dark suits in between.

And then there was him, isolated from the actual investigation, an observer on what should still be his case. He was convinced the explosion was connected to Cranesbrook.

"Hey, you got nothing better to do than hang out on the waterfront in the middle of the night?"

Detective Dean Farrell appeared, looking slightly rumpled as usual. He'd barely run a comb through his salt-and-pepper hair and his tie wore remnants of food.

"You know me," Rand said. "I never could stay away from a party."

"Where's the kegger?"

"They won't let me at it."

Farrell snorted. "Yeah, tough break. They're not gonna let you at anything for a while, not until you get shrunk."

An automatic result of an offender getting killed rather than being brought in. Rand had no regrets for taking out Vanderhoven. He'd done what he'd needed to do. Despite Vanderhoven's so-called power—amplifying other people's emotions until they couldn't think straight—Zoe was safe and back in Echo's arms.

Rand wondered if Bray had the same special power of Vanderhoven or Darnell. Or if his brain had developed in some other direction.

Not that he could discuss this with Farrell. No one else in the department knew about the crazy side effects of the lab accident.

"So you think this explosion has something to do with whatever's going on at Cranesbrook?" Farrell asked.

"Take a look around you. At the vehicles."

"Yeah?"

"Notice anything?"

"An assortment of brown-and-white cop mobiles."

"And one black Corvette," Rand said. "You want to guess who owns it?"

"Someone at Cranesbrook?"

"Formerly."

"Not Sloane?"

"Yes, Sloane." Rand shook his head. "The moment I saw it, I knew—"

"What? You think he's in the drink?"

"I think he had the knowledge and probably the means to set that explosion."

He should have stayed in bed with Echo. But the moment the call had come in from a local to inform him that Claire Fanshaw's residence had just gone boom, he'd had to see what was what for himself. He'd left an exhausted Echo and baby Zoe snuggled together fast asleep and had come running.

The black Corvette had been waiting there, mocking him. He'd seen it at Sloane's place and now here it was at the scene of the crime.

Now it looked as though he was going to have to tell the woman he loved that her brother was every bit as guilty as he'd feared. The state cops had put out an APB on Sloane, but Rand wasn't so sure the bastard would be found alive.

"If Sloane blew up the boat, why'd he leave his wheels?" Farrell mused.

"Could've been caught in his own explosion."

But a couple of hours later, when the divers came out of the water, they seemed disappointed they hadn't found any spare parts.

No human remains.

No Sloane.

Had he developed gills or something? Or had he been too close, turned into a human pink mist that floated away on the wind?

What they *had* found was a twisted piece of black metal—something that might have been in the shape of a box with a metal bowl built in the top.

"What do you make of it?" he asked the fire marshal.

"Looks something like a flashpot to me. You know, for creating special effects on a stage or in the movies. But this one probably held plastic explosives— Semtex or C-4."

"On a stage or in the movies," Rand repeated. "Any other place you'd find a flashpot? What about a science lab like the ones at Cranesbrook Associates?"

"Yeah, I suppose. The woman living on the boat works there, right?"

"She does, but not in a lab. She's a computer specialist."

"Looks like she made some serious enemy."

Rand wondered what exactly Claire Fanshaw knew that Brayden Sloane wanted her silenced for good.

His brain is on fire. Burning. Melting.

The sun bakes him and dries his mouth. He keeps an eye out for the enemy as he signals the others to head for the Humvee.

The kid explodes in his face.

Another explosion...another victim...guy in a white lab coat sprawls across the floor.

"I can't get enough of you." A hoarse whisper from the blonde under him. "Ride me hard. You're it, exactly what I need."

Liar. She needs her husband.

"I'll be back, son. Two days, three max."

Day after day, he watches out the window in vain.

Then the redhead smiles that smile. "I'm your wife. I want you more than anything."

Her lips move but he can't hear her over the lie.

She tugs at him, traps him, then plunges her fist into his chest and pulls out part of him, bloody and still beating. He reaches for her, but she fades like the vision she is.

His brain is on fire. Burning. Melting. The flames threatening to devour him until he is no more.

He fights it. He has to be all right. Has to be.

For the people who died. For the future victims if Project Cypress isn't stopped.

For Echo and Zoe…and for Claire…

BRAY'S EYES FLASHED open, his gaze lighting on Claire's face. She looked relaxed, innocent in sleep. He touched her lips and willed her to be honest with him. Willed her to tell him why she'd concocted this man-and-wife charade. Willed her to want him for real.

Only then would he be all right.

"I NEED TO SEE my sister."

Bray had been waiting to talk this over with Claire since dawn. The hour had dragged by, feeling like several, but he hadn't wanted to wake her.

Claire pushed herself into a sitting position, wedged her back against the driver's seat and stretched. "Do you think that's wise?"

Mesmerized for a moment by her beautiful dishevelment—a look that bade him to take her back to bed—Bray got himself in control. He couldn't be distracted. He needed to be on his game.

"I don't care if it's wise or not," he said. "Someone is out to kill us. Next time I might not get away with my skin. I need to see Echo and tell her face-to-face that I don't know what's happening or why her baby was taken. I can't let her think I had anything to do with Zoe's kidnapping."

Claire frowned. "Vanderhoven was the kidnapper. She knows that."

"But I was the ransom. She might think I was involved with…with I don't even know what. If I tell her I didn't have anything to do with what happened, she'll believe me."

"Are you sure?"

"She knows how I feel about lies."

Claire's eyes widened slightly, but she covered quickly. Her voice was a little thick when she asked, "Sounds like you don't like them."

"I hate them," he said honestly, and watched the pulse in her throat suddenly tick. "I've hated them since Echo and I were kids and our dad told us he was going away for a few days and never came back." He silently bade her to be honest with him, to end his uncertainty with her. "I used to stand at the window watching for him every day after school until it got dark."

"I'm sure he meant to come back."

"No, he never did. He abandoned us and made a little sucker of me. It took me nearly a year to come to terms with that, but finally I had to. I swore I would never have feelings for anyone else who lied to me, but I made the mistake a second time." The memory was as sharp as if it had happened days ago rather than years ago. "I thought she was a gift, someone sent to save me."

"A woman?"

He nodded. "In Afghanistan. Her name was Krystal. I met her the night I saw my mate step on that land mine."

"You were vulnerable."

"Hell, I was drunk. I thought I could lose myself in her. In the morning she was gone. I figured I would never see her again."

"But you did."

"That night. And the night after that. I got caught up in her, thought of her as my lifeline. I didn't ask any personal questions about her and she didn't volunteer any personal information—like the fact that she was married."

"Maybe she thought you knew."

"I should have guessed. Maybe on some level I had. You don't find many women like that in Afghanistan. I was too screwed around to realize it, though."

"How did she get there? Surely wives aren't allowed in combat areas."

"Reporters are. She got herself assigned to be near her husband. She had a few days off and came on base to see him. Captain Jack Hansen. Apparently it wasn't a positive reunion. He didn't approve of her being in a war zone, reporter or not. He went out on a mission and told her to get back to the States. She found me instead. And then the captain found us together. I was in the brig faster than anyone could ask me my side of the story."

"But they didn't court-martial you."

"Because Gage spoke up for me. He intervened, told Captain Hansen how I'd gotten twisted around by what happened on that recon mission. The captain agreed not to press charges if I would cut my tour of duty short. Krystal threatened them with bad publicity if they didn't look the other way. Luckily, the military didn't need any more negative press, so I didn't go to trial."

"She doesn't sound like a bad person. She did stand up for you."

"If she hadn't lied in the first place, I wouldn't have been in the brig." Pausing for a moment, he wondered what it would take to make Claire tell the truth. "Lies don't bother you?"

"It all depends. Sometimes a person has a really good reason to lie."

Undoubtedly she meant herself. "What kind of a reason would it take for *you* to lie, Claire?"

"We're not talking about me."

No, she didn't want to talk about the lies she'd spun around him. Until she came clean with him and admitted that she'd tricked him into thinking they were married, how could he be certain anything she said to him was the truth? He couldn't trust her.

"So how much of your memory is back?" she asked. "That was pretty detailed stuff you just shared."

"The long term memory is starting to flow. Short-term is different. I only remember a few seconds of the lab accident—those few seconds that keep haunting my dreams." When she didn't respond, he said, "Now back to my sister…"

In the end, Bray agreed to call Echo rather than surprise her. It was a better idea anyway. With the kidnapping and all, he had no idea who might be hanging around her place. He might be the one surprised.

While Claire changed inside the CRV into workout

clothes, he sat outside the vehicle on a tree stump and used the cell phone he'd bought in Annapolis to call Echo.

"Hello, Rand?" came a voice that proved to be hearteningly familiar.

"It's Bray."

"Oh, my God, Bray! You're alive!" Joy filled Echo's voice. "Where are you? Are you all right?"

"I'm fine. Well, mostly."

"Where have you been? Why haven't you called me before this?"

"I've been having a little trouble with my memory since the lab accident. Until the day before yesterday, I didn't even know who I was."

Echo made a choked sound. "I knew something was wrong! Have you seen a doctor?"

"I was checked out in Baltimore."

"How did you get there? Are you there now?"

"Whoa. I'll answer all your questions, at least what I can, but how about I do it in person? I want to see you and Zoe. I'm in the area."

"How soon can you get here?"

"Your place might not be the best," he said, still thinking of the authorities surprising them. "How about we meet at Waterside Café in about an hour for breakfast?"

"I'll be there with Zoe."

Bray clicked off, wondering if he would really remember his sister fully or if a veil of uncertainty would remain between them. His memory was returning in bits and pieces and he didn't even need to touch anything to remember some incident. But there were still blanks, particularly concerning Cranesbrook Associates.

The net was closing in, tightening. Now he not only had the authorities after him, but someone who wanted him dead.

He only hoped he could fill in the gaps before it was too late.

Chapter Twelve

As they drove up to the restaurant, Claire began to panic. She hadn't been able to talk Bray out of this meeting with his sister. Part of her wanted to do the cowardly thing and let him go in alone, but she had feelings for the man, and if Echo was going to slap him with the truth about their relationship, she needed to be there. She would take the fallout, and she would try to make it right.

So why couldn't she do it now?

A coward. She was a real coward, fearful that Bray would look at her with disgust and shut her out of his life forever.

Echo was waiting for them at a table in back, away from other diners, with Zoe next to her in a high chair. Zoe's eyes were pale like her mother's and her fine brown hair was just starting to curl in wisps around her round face. Thankfully she'd been rescued unhurt. Claire was certain she would be in her mother's line of sight from now until young adulthood, at least.

When Echo saw Bray, her face lit then crumpled as she started to cry. She nearly knocked over her chair as she got to her feet and moved toward her brother, her lavender angel-sleeved tunic fluttering. She threw her arms around him as though she would never let him go, either.

"Oh, Bray, I was so afraid for you. I thought…well, the worst."

"That I was guilty?"

"No of course not, I never thought that. I was worried that you were hurt…or dead." Echo let go of him and looked over his shoulder, her expression questioning. "Claire?"

"Hi, Echo. I'm sorry I didn't tell you about Bray when you came by yesterday," Claire quickly said. "He was on *Lainie's Moor,* asleep. If you hadn't been with Detective McClellan, I would have brought you in."

Bray's voice went stiff when he said, "You didn't tell me you saw my sister."

"It must have slipped my mind."

Claire gave Echo an expression that pleaded for her understanding. And her discretion. She could see the other woman's mind working as she tried to figure out the relationship. Claire placed her hand on Bray's arm and Echo's eyebrows rose. She got the connection.

Bray smiled down at Zoe and ran a gentle finger along her cheek. The baby smiled at him, threw her chubby arms in the air and crowed. Obviously she recognized him even if Bray didn't really know her, Claire thought. As they sat, the waitress arrived with a pot of coffee. She took their breakfast orders and left again.

The moment they were alone, Echo said, "Bray, the authorities think you had something to do with the lab accident at Cranesbrook. I know you would never do anything dishonest, but I haven't even been able to convince Rand—"

"Rand?"

"Detective McClellan," Claire clarified.

Bray frowned at his sister. "You and this detective…?"

Echo nodded. "I—I love him, Bray, and he loves me. If you give yourself up to him, he'll help clear your name. He'll do that for me."

"Even though he thinks I'm guilty."

"But you aren't. Tell him everything you know and you'll convince him."

"That's the problem, Echo. I don't know anything. Or not enough. My memory was wiped out and it's just now starting to come back. That's why I disappeared. Until two days ago, when Zoe was kidnapped and my photo was on the front page of the *Baltimore Sun,* I didn't even know who I was. I don't make a very convincing witness for myself."

Claire said, "*I* believe you."

"That's because you're—"

"On your side," she quickly cut in, stopping him from calling her his wife in front of Echo.

Bray brought his sister up to date on how he'd gotten to Baltimore and his stay in a homeless shelter, things he hadn't even shared with Claire. He told her about hitching to St. Stephens and about his using subterfuge to get back into the Cranesbrook labs.

At which point Claire stiffened.

But rather than going into how they'd bumped into each other two nights before, Bray merely said, "Unfortunately, I didn't find anything that jogged my memory about what happened. They'd already cleared out the lab and storeroom, of course."

"About the storeroom." Echo shifted uncomfortably. "They have footage of you in there on the day of the accident."

"I really don't remember."

"It's time-stamped an hour before the explosion. They said you had no reason to be in there. I have a copy on DVD in my bag. We have to find a way for you to see it."

"No problem," Claire said. "We can use my laptop to check it out before we leave."

Echo gave Claire an intent once-over again, but she kept her questions to herself.

The food arrived. Starving, Claire dug right in, as did Bray. Echo picked at her food, then lifted a fussy Zoe out of her chair and held her tight. The baby sucked her thumb and fisted her mother's hair with her free hand. Claire could see the tears form in Echo's eyes. She blinked back tears of her own and concentrated on her food.

"Bray, I'm really afraid for you," Echo said. "I don't know what the authorities will do if they spot you on the street. You need to give yourself up."

Claire felt Bray's tension when he asked, "So they can lock me up?"

"At least you'll be alive until they can sort this thing out. It'll look better for you if you turn yourself over to the authorities and tell them what you know."

"That's the problem. I can't give them anything new. And if as you say they have proof that I was in the storeroom, that doesn't look good for me, does it?"

"Maybe you *can* give them something new." Echo hesitated a moment, then in a rush asked, "Has anything unusual happened to you since the accident?"

Bray put down his fork. "Like what?"

"Both Gage and Vanderhoven were affected by the chemicals." Echo lowered her voice. "Their minds were affected. I guess you could say 'expanded.'"

"We know," Claire said. "Gage made some notes in the Cranesbrook computer files about what was going on. He said he could open doors with his mind."

"And move other things," Echo said. "They call it telekinesis."

"What about Vanderhoven?"

"Not the same. He was able to amplify people's emotions so they lost control. What about *you*, Bray?"

"I can't do either of those things, not that I know of. But I can pick up memories by touching objects," he admitted. "Other people's memories."

"I don't understand," Echo murmured. "How can the chemicals work so differently on different people? What did the Department of Defense hope to do with this weapon of theirs?"

So she'd been correct, Claire thought. The DOD was responsible for Project Cypress, and Cranesbrook was inventing some sort of weapon.

"Maybe it's not doing what it was meant to do." That was the only thing that made sense to Claire. "Something went wrong and someone at Cranesbrook is trying to cover it up so they don't lose millions."

"But surely the authorities know about the powers Gage and Vanderhoven developed," Bray said.

Echo shook her head. "Only Rand, as far as I know.

It's not something a person believes in lightly. They kind of have to see proof."

Just as she had, Claire thought.

"So will you do it?" Echo asked. "Will you give yourself up? Show them what you can do?"

"It wouldn't prove anything, Echo, certainly not that I'm innocent of wrongdoing. They might think I knew what the chemicals would do and purposely set them off."

Echo sank into silence and clung to her now sleeping daughter. A lump settled in Claire's stomach and she set down her fork, unable to finish her breakfast.

Bray seemed to have removed himself from the gathering. He kept eating but waved the waitress over and asked for the check. When it came, Claire insisted on using her credit card to pay so if the authorities were tracking his, they wouldn't know he was on the Eastern Shore. Bray didn't fight her for it.

Moments later, they were on their way out of the restaurant, heading for Claire's CRV and her laptop.

Bray stopped to get a newspaper from a box. Would the boat explosion be front-page news? If Echo already knew about it, she hadn't indicated such.

Pushing Zoe's stroller, Echo kept up with her and softly asked, "What's going on between you and my brother?"

"Nothing bad, I promise you." Claire glanced back to see him scanning the front page. "I care for Bray and want to help him clear his name."

"Is that all?"

"What other motive would I have?" Claire asked, this lie nearly choking her.

Claire could tell Echo wasn't buying her innocent act, but thankfully, she let the subject drop, at least for the moment. Bray caught up to them as Claire opened the car doors with her remote. She climbed into the driver's seat, put the key in the ignition, started the car and connected the laptop adaptor to the vehicle's lighter socket.

"It'll take just a minute for my laptop to fire up."

"That gives me a minute to reconnect with my niece." He turned to his sister. "Can I hold Zoe? I'm happy she isn't scared of me."

"How could she be scared of the first man who ever held her?" Echo said, sounding a little choked.

Revving up the laptop, Claire glanced up to see Bray take Zoe into his arms. The baby squealed and smacked him in the nose with an open hand. Bray's expression softened as he looked into his niece's face. And Claire's throat tightened as she thought how comfortable Bray looked holding a baby.

"Here's the DVD," Echo said, offering the disk to her.

"Thanks." Claire took it, waited until her computer's operating system was humming comfortably, then popped in the disk. She set the laptop on the dash so they could all see. "Here we go."

The footage opened with an empty lab, but then a shadow appeared on the monitor. A man followed. As he strode toward the storeroom, his spiked black hair glistened in the overhead lights. He pulled the door open and, pausing, looked over his shoulder toward the camera as if checking to make sure he wasn't being watched before disappearing inside.

"That's me, all right."

A black band ran under the image. The time, date and lab number were branded in red.

"And that's the day…" Claire murmured. "Maybe an hour before the accident."

"Does this help you remember anything?" Echo asked.

Bray's expression tightened. "Nope. Not a thing."

Noticing his forehead pulling together in a deep frown, Claire asked, "What is it?"

"Play it back."

They watched the sequence again as Bray came into the shot, then walked into the storeroom.

"Something seems off, but I can't quite place it."

"What kind of something?" Claire asked.

"Something about the way I'm dressed."

Echo said, "I don't get it."

"I don't, either."

"Wait," Claire murmured. "I have it. It's not the clothing. The radio. It's wrong. It's in a sleeve attached to your belt."

"And that would be wrong why?" Echo asked.

Bray answered, "Because the radio should be attached to the shirt pocket. I remember now. We used to carry the larger radios but switched to the smaller units last spring."

Claire nodded. "He's right. I've never seen them any other way. Could someone have tampered with the footage to throw suspicion on him?"

Bray asked his sister, "Where did you get the DVD?"

"Rand made a copy from the original, which he got from Hank Riddell."

"Riddell again!" Claire gasped. "Yesterday morning he found one of the janitors who'd just died of a heart attack. Then I caught him searching my desk. He said he was looking for a folder for Dr. Ulrich. The folder was in plain sight on top, and he was searching through my drawers."

"What kind of work does Riddell do on Project Cypress?" Bray mused.

Claire shrugged. "Considering we can't get to the files, who knows exactly other than the men on the project. Riddell is Ulrich's and Kelso's research fellow. Wes Vanderhoven worked on the project as a lab assistant. And so did Mac Ellroy. Mac left under mysterious circumstances, and Vanderhoven is dead."

Before they could discuss it further, a midnight-blue Crown Victoria entered the lot and with a screech of tires, stopped yards from them. Claire's eyes widened when she realized the driver was none other than Detective Rand McClellan.

She shut down the laptop, closed the cover and slipped the computer into the back seat.

The detective flew from the car, yelling, "Brayden Sloane, stop right there!"

Chapter Thirteen

Stepping out of her vehicle, Claire couldn't believe Echo had arranged for the detective to be there. She could see that Bray was equally disbelieving when he gave his sister an accusing look.

"You called in the cops?"

"Not the cops. Just Rand. He's on our side. I left a voice mail for him to meet us here to talk." A desperate-sounding Echo white-knuckled the stroller handle. "I had to do it for your sake. I'm so afraid for you, Bray. Too many people connected with the Cranesbrook accident have died already. I don't want you to be next."

But the men ignored her. They were too focused on each other. Claire noted their hard expressions and aggressive stances.

So who was more macho?

Rand stepped closer to Bray, saying, "You and I need to have a serious conversation, Sloane, starting with that boat blowing up last night."

"What boat?" Echo asked, her panic spreading to Zoe, who started to cry.

Bray turned away, saying, "Talking isn't going to

get us anywhere." But Rand grabbed him by the arm to stop him.

Big mistake.

One look at Bray's expression made Claire go cold as ice.

"Why don't we go back inside?" she said. "Have some more coffee."

Bray shrugged off the detective's hold and continued moving toward the CRV.

"Stop, Sloane. Now."

"The hell I will. C'mon, Claire."

"Don't walk away from me, Sloane," Rand warned, reaching out and grabbing Bray's elbow with one hand, his wrist with the other.

Before Rand could use the leverage to trap him, Bray reacted. He turned and slashed the side of his hand at Rand's, the sharp jolt making the detective let go. Then Bray was on him, shoving him hard with both hands and not looking as though he was going to back down.

Claire nearly panicked when she saw Rand reach for his holster.

"Rand, no!" Echo cried. Zoe screamed in response until her mother picked her up out of the stroller.

Claire couldn't believe this was happening.

Moving fast as Rand pulled his gun, Bray shifted, whirled and kicked out. His foot connected with Rand's hand and kicked away the weapon before he lunged for the man, who stormed, "Don't be a damn fool, Sloane!"

Hearing Bray mumble something about the enemy, Claire felt her pulse lurch. He was in military mode and, in his mind, engaged in hand-to-hand combat. Rand had a few good moves, but he wasn't driven by nightmares and desperation. God forbid Bray should actually hurt a police officer, not to mention the man his sister loved.

"Bray, stop. Calm down, please."

Her words did nothing.

"Stop, both of you," Echo pleaded, clinging to her baby as the men traded punches. "This wasn't supposed to happen."

The men got into a body hold and danced in a circle. Rand was fit and trained as a police officer, but Claire feared he was no match for a half-deranged, ex-Special Ops soldier who was all muscle.

Realizing that Bray didn't seem connected with the present, she was reminded of the night before on the pier, when something inside Bray's mind gave way to the past.

She tried to get between them. Bray threw out his arm and swept her away with no more trouble than he would a fly. She landed on her butt on the ground. And when Bray's sharp elbow caught Rand in the solar plexis, the detective landed almost next to her, gasping for air. Bray was immediately on top of him, arm raised, knuckles poised toward Rand's throat.

"Rand's not the enemy!" Claire screamed at him. "Bray, stop now before you kill him!"

Bray's arm froze in midair.

"It's all right, Bray. Back off. You have to back off."

Claire wrapped a hand around that arm and pulled it out of striking position.

Bray seemed confused as he came back to the present. Blinking, he looked from Rand to his sister, then got to his feet. "Let's get out of here."

"No, wait," Echo said. "At least talk to Rand, please."

"It's too late for talking."

Bray was already pushing Claire into the vehicle. He kept pushing until she crossed into the passenger seat. The engine was still running from when she'd connected the computer. He didn't even close the driver's door until after he drove off.

Claire looked out the back window. Rand was getting to his feet. Thankfully, the detective seemed to be all right, though she was certain Bray had made no new friend or supporter on this day.

FEELING AS IF A STORM cloud were wrapped around his head, he strolled through the exhibit building of the St. Stephens Maritime Museum. He'd thought the excursion might provide some distraction, a way to get his dark mood under control. When he'd seen the morning newspaper, he'd almost gone ballistic, had almost given himself away.

Instead of being a soothing experience, the screams and shrieks of the little kids in the museum had exacerbated his headache—and therefore his anger—until both threatened to spin out of control. He needed to learn to channel his anger, to subdue it when he didn't require it.

When two kids running through the hall to the toilets collided with his legs, he thought he might explode.

"A sea dragon's going to eat you both," he snarled, already thinking about it after checking to make certain there was no one else close by.

The little girl sticking out her tongue did it, made him lose his temper. His brain flared with heat and he could feel the pulse rushing through him. Suddenly a sea dragon rose up out of the mists rising from the floor. Both kids ran away screaming.

He let out his breath and let go of the image, and the sea dragon dissipated. Let the little harridan tell her mommy what she saw. Her mother would put it to a child's imagination. The kid was lucky he hadn't done worse to her.

He'd been practicing. A lot. He enjoyed freaking people out. His sense of power grew with each incident, and he wondered, given enough time, what he could do with the power.

Money was no longer enough for him. He didn't care what the hell happened to the project. He wasn't interested in sharing his power. He didn't even have to get angry for the images to appear anymore. He merely needed to concentrate and he could make anyone see anything he conjured up.

As far as he could tell, the only flies in the ointment were Sloane and Darnell. And Claire Fanshaw. What the hell was her involvement? He'd been pondering it but hadn't been able to figure it out.

Being thwarted didn't sit well with him. His plan had been perfect. Get rid of both Sloane and the woman with one little explosion. So why hadn't they been there, back at the boat, by midnight?

His anger surged.

As he left the museum and walked out into the sunlight, a homeless guy came right up to him, hand out.

"Spare change, mister?"

"Get out of my way." He shouldered past the piece of

human excrement, nearly knocking the man to the ground.

With a loud yell, the man lunged forward, grabbed his shoulder and whipped him around. "Hey, who do you think you are?"

"Someone you don't mess with."

Knowing the homeless guy would be afraid of the police rounding him up and throwing him in the tank, he conjured one of St. Stephens' boys in blue.

"Officer!" he called, waving the vision over.

The "cop" came running, reaching for his gun.

The homeless guy freaked and ran straight into the street where a car coming from the parking lot plowed into him with a thud and a screech of brakes.

"Hey, that guy got hit!" someone said.

Suddenly people were rushing out from everywhere, clustering around the fallen man.

One woman said, "I just saw a cop. Where'd he go?"

Smiling as a plan of action to take care of Sloane and the woman came to him, he turned his back on the accident and left the scene.

BRAY DROVE UNTIL the anger wore off, though it took a while considering his own sister had set a trap for him. He got almost all the way to Route 50 before pulling off at some creek at the outskirts of Easton, the next town up from St. Stephens.

As if she could read his still-disturbed thoughts, Claire murmured, "You know Echo was just trying to help, right? She's afraid for you."

"Great way she has of showing it. I could have been shot."

Throwing himself from the car, he walked down to the water's edge. A white-tailed deer that had been drinking ran for a stand of trees, and a small flock of black ducks swam a safe distance away before stopping to sun themselves.

Claire caught up to him and stood quietly for a moment before saying, "Detective McClellan wouldn't have drawn his gun if you had just talked to him."

"You don't know that."

"And you don't know that he would have." Claire seemed hesitant, then asked, "Have you always had trouble controlling your anger?"

"It's the situation."

"Are you sure of that? You were pretty intense before the accident. I saw you go off a couple of times at Cranesbrook Associates."

Bray thought about it. He *had* been having trouble keeping his temper for a while now. He'd been walking around all tight inside, a situation that he thought had developed a few months back. And then something came to him.

"There was a break-in at an apartment complex that Five Star covers in St. Stephens," he said. "The office called it in and since I was so close, I went to investigate. I caught the guy red-handed. He had a weapon. But that's where my memory of what happened ends. I vaguely remember later the guy threatening to sue me for injuries. I must have lost it."

"A trigger," Claire mused.

"As in a gun?"

"As in an incident that brought back a trauma you buried long ago."

"You're talking about Post Traumatic Stress Disorder."

"Afghanistan made you a ripe candidate, don't you think? Maybe the guy at the apartment complex attacked you and on some level reminded you of the unspeakable things you saw when you were in the military."

"That was five years ago."

"It happens. You could be better than most at burying what you don't want to face."

Bray had heard of guys who seemed okay suddenly going off half-cocked. Is that what had happened to him?

Claire went on. "And then there was the lab accident at Cranesbrook—an explosion—and all of a sudden your memory is gone."

"Are you saying you think my amnesia is self-induced?"

"Not self-induced, but related. What happened in the lab could have triggered earlier memories. You're going to have to deal with it all sometime, Bray. You should get professional help."

"I fight my battles alone."

"That's the problem. You've gone against everything you learned in the military, haven't you? Didn't you depend on the men who watched your back?"

"What good does that do someone who steps on a land mine?"

Claire moved in close to him, as though giving him her support. Her mere touch took him from anger to wanting to take her in his arms. Wife or not, she could be irresistible; he couldn't get enough of her. It took all his willpower not to do what he wanted this time.

"It's not your fault," she said softly. "Your buddy didn't die because of you."

On one level, Bray knew that. But on another…

"Morgan. His name was Taureen Morgan."

"You remembered," she murmured.

"I'm remembering a lot of things."

He stared down into Claire's beautiful green eyes, willing her to open up to him the way he just had to her, willing her to tell him the truth. Something in her face told him she wanted to, but in the end, her expression clouded and a purposeful smile curved her lips.

Bray's gut went tight.

"The question is, what do we do next?" she asked. "The most important thing we need to make happen is to clear your name."

"Which means learning more about Project Cypress."

He stepped away from her, but even distance didn't settle him down inside.

"It's probably all there, in those computer files," Claire mused. "You should have gotten me that security clearance when I asked for it."

Why had she wanted that clearance anyway? Bray wondered. Apparently not for legitimate work purposes. He suspected she'd had some reason for working at Cranesbrook other than a paycheck. The name Mac Ellroy came to mind and he pushed down the foreign emotion surging through him.

He asked, "How could I have given security clearance on Project Cypress to you, when Gage and I were denied that particular clearance ourselves?"

Another memory.

They were flooding back to him now in fits and starts. There were still gaps. Too many. But certainly not as many as there had been even the day before. All it had taken was putting him back in familiar surroundings for him to regain his past.

Claire looked at him closely, as if she had a plan. "The answer lies with one of three men—Kelso, Ulrich or Riddell. Maybe if you could call up *their* memories…"

"Unless you have a Project Cypress collection for me to play with, that doesn't sound like it would be easy. We'd have to get back inside the compound, and that might be tricky, at least for you. Your clearances might already be wiped out."

Claire shook her head. "It's still the weekend, so it's not as though I haven't shown up for work. And while the boat blew up, they didn't find my remains. So people would assume I'm still alive."

"People who want you dead."

"*Someone* wants me dead. That doesn't mean everyone associated with Cranesbrook does. And the mastermind behind all this mayhem might not be a person with the power to change my clearances. I'm thinking Hank Riddell." Claire's voice hardened as she ticked off her points on her fingers. One… "He showed up at Beech Grove Clinic after the accident." Two… "I found him searching my desk." Three… "And now we learn he turned over to the authorities that DVD with footage edited to place you in Lab 7 when you weren't there."

"Riddell does seem a likely candidate. But isn't he a little green behind the ears to pull this off himself? Didn't you say he was friends with Martin Kelso?"

"I think Kelso is the one who got him hired."

"If Kelso's involved, we're screwed."

"Maybe. Even if he is, my thought is he wouldn't do anything to make himself look suspicious. The boat I'm living on blows up and then he pulls my clearance… I don't think so. We should do it, get back into Cranesbrook. If you touch the right objects, you might remember what happened in Lab 7."

"And recapture memories of whoever was responsible for the accident." He thought about it for a moment. "Tonight. Late. And backup wouldn't hurt."

"You don't think Detective McClellan is going to be doing you any favors after your last encounter."

"Not McClellan. Gage. I need to find my partner for a face-to-face, tell him in person what I know…and what I don't."

"How, when we don't have any idea where he is?"

"Actually, we do. *I* do. He's got Lily stashed in a bed-and-breakfast at Rehoboth Beach."

"How do you know that? One of your visions?"

He nodded. "At Five Star."

"And you didn't say anything? Nice, Bray."

He caught her gaze. "Omission isn't as bad as lying."

She looked away first and started back toward the vehicle. "We'd better get going. Looks like we have another day of driving in front of us."

But at the end of that day, Bray hoped they would have their answers, along with a way to clear his name and proof to bring the villain responsible to justice.

And then what for him?

Back to Baltimore and Five Star?

Without Claire?

Chapter Fourteen

"It's okay, my little sweetheart, we're home now," Echo whispered in Zoe's ear.

Tired beyond fussy, the baby was sucking on her thumb and pulling on a hank of her mother's hair. Echo held Zoe close and removed a bag of groceries from the trunk of her car. She'd retrieved the junker from the garage, then had done some minimal grocery shopping.

Quickly heading for the house, she nearly tripped when she heard a familiar voice say, "Echo, you're finally home."

Whirling around, she came face-to-face with her brother's business partner. Where in the world had he come from? Glancing over his shoulder, she noticed a car with darkened windows parked at the curb.

"Gage, what are you doing here? Where's Lily?"

Gage Darnell's dark eyes bored into her intently, and his military-cut hair seemed to bristle with his tension. "I saw the news about the boat blowing up and Bray being suspected of doing it. He needs my help to clear his name."

"Oh, thank God." Echo breathed a sigh of relief.

After the fight that morning, she couldn't count on Rand looking kindly at her brother, no matter his promise to try to clear Bray. "He can't do this alone. He doesn't even have his memory back."

"His memory… So that's why he went missing for so long."

Echo unlocked the door. "Let's go inside. I need to put Zoe down for her nap."

"Go ahead."

Echo set the groceries on the hall table and took Zoe straight to her bedroom with its yellow walls and equally colorful pictures of balloons. The baby was already asleep, so Echo put her directly in her crib and covered her. She smoothed the fine hair from the little face and felt her chest tighten the same way she did every time she realized she could have lost her daughter for good.

Taking a shaky breath, Echo refused to believe she would lose anyone she loved. Not Zoe, not Rand—he would get over the fight they'd had when she'd held him back from going after her brother—and not Bray himself. Her brother had always been there for her. Surely she could do *something* to help clear his name.

She rushed out of Zoe's room to find Gage still standing in the entrance to the house. "Come in. Sit."

"I wish I had the time to be sociable, but I need to get a move on. I have some things I want to check out, so I'm in kind of a hurry."

"About Bray…do you have a plan to clear him?"

"Not yet, but I have a lead. And I want to see what he knows."

Echo shook her head. "Like I said, not much. He

hasn't remembered anything to help himself. Well, other than what he got through his power."

"Power? So he does have one."

"Not telekinesis or anything to do with emotions."

"What, then? How can it help him?"

"Memories," Echo said, "just not his own memories. When he touches an object, it's like he relives what happened to it in the past."

Appearing to zero in on that information, Gage said, "So all he needs to do is to touch the right objects and he'll have the answers to everything."

"Yeah, but he needs to *get* to the right objects. That's the problem. Who knows if they even exist anymore?"

Gage thought about it for a moment, then asked, "Can you get a message to Bray for me?"

"Yes, of course."

Echo hoped Bray would pick up his cell when he saw it was her calling him. She'd picked up the number of his new cell phone when he'd called her that morning.

"Then tell him to meet me at the Landsdale lighthouse tonight at eight. It's closed for the season, so it's a safe bet no one will be around to see him."

"All right. I wish there was more I could do."

"Leave it to me, Echo. I'll take care of Bray, I promise."

Echo nodded and watched Gage walk off.

She started to close the door, then thought to give him her cell number so he could reach him no matter what, but when she looked for him, he'd already vanished.

CLAIRE'S LIES were scaring her. Bray's memory seemed to be coming back in waves. How long before he realized she'd been playing him?

Her lies had created acceptable worlds for her to live in without having people feel sorry for her. The best mother in the world. The best home. The greatest dad. All lies. Lies had helped her get out of some chancy situations, too. Gang members who'd been hassling her. A guy at school coming on to her who wouldn't take no for an answer. A convenience store robbery she'd once interrupted.

Her lies had never been meant to hurt anyone, and as far as she knew, they never had before. But this time was different. Bray was different. Vulnerable. He'd come to think of her as an important part of his life.

When he realized she wasn't, then what?

Claire couldn't stand contemplating the what-ifs. Couldn't stand thinking about a life without Bray being part of it. How had this happened? They'd only been together a few days. She guessed the attraction had been there between them from the first time they'd clashed at Cranesbrook. Being thrown together 24/7 had been like a whole series of dangerous dates strung together. Whatever the explanation, she was hooked. The lump in her throat was simply too big to swallow.

"I think that's it up ahead," Bray said, indicating a three-story white house with a sprawling columned veranda decked with containers of flowers. "Sunrise Bed and Breakfast."

"I don't care about the breakfast, but I bet they give great bed," Claire said with a wistful sigh. "After spending the night in the back of this vehicle, I'm acquainted with muscles I didn't even know I had."

"Which might not be from the sleeping part," he said, his tone momentarily teasing. "Don't get your fantasies up. This is a hit-and-run mission. I talk to Gage, we form a plan and then we head out and execute it."

Claire groaned in disappointment and tried not to think of how romantic as well as comfortable it might be for her and Bray to share the bed that she now couldn't get off her mind. A comfortable mattress, fluffy pillows, a sea breeze rolling in the windows. Perhaps some quiet time with Bray on a couple of the veranda rockers or walking hand-in-hand on the beach, which was less than a block away.

She'd only known Bray in the biblical sense for a few days. Fool that she was, she'd gotten caught in her own web. Who knew trying to get the truth about Mac would end her up in this predicament. Here she'd gone and fallen in love with the man she'd been using to get information she still didn't have.

And now the truth was certain to come out when they faced Gage and Lily Darnell.

Why hadn't she gotten out of this when she still could?

"I don't see Gage's Jeep," Bray said, suddenly sounding tense.

"Maybe he took Lily on some excursion for the day."

Which meant she and Bray would be cooling their heels for who knew how long. Maybe they could get a room, and a shower, after all. A reprieve of sorts.

"Or they already checked out." Bray pulled into a parking spot across the street from the B & B. "Maybe I should have called first."

"A little late for regrets. Let's go in and see if they're still registered."

Entering the B & B, they were quickly approached by a young brunette who was coming down the staircase. She wore brown capris, a bronze sweater topped by a matching shrug and a welcoming smile.

"Good afternoon. Do you have reservations with us?" she asked Bray.

"Uh, no—"

"I'm sorry, we're fully booked."

"We don't want to stay here," he told her. "We just want to know if Gage and Lily Darnell are still here."

The brunette's expression changed to one of caution. "I'm sorry, but we can't share guest information. The Privacy Act, you know."

"I'm not asking for information *about* them," Bray said. "I just want to know if they're still here."

It was obvious that the Darnells were still guests, so when the brunette still balked, Claire said, "Please, my husband hasn't seen his sister in nearly a year. We flew into Baltimore to surprise Lily and Gage for their anniversary, and we're the ones who got surprised. Can't you just call up to their room and tell them Bray is here to see them? Please?"

The last "please" seemed to get to the woman. She nodded. "All right, I'll call up. You wait right here."

"Tell them Bray *and* Claire," Claire called after her.

When the brunette was out of earshot, Bray said, "Brother? Anniversary?"

"You weren't getting anywhere with her. Sometimes you just have to know how to handle people who don't want to give you what you need."

"Interesting take on life. Not everyone would agree with it, though. Especially not the people being handled."

"Everyone does it in some way. Not telling someone about a special event because they're not invited and you don't want hurt feelings. Pretending a blow-out with a family member was just a little disagreement. Telling people what they want to hear. All of that stuff that doesn't mean anything in the big picture. My saying that you're Lily's brother isn't hurting anything."

"If you lie often enough, don't you get confused? How do you keep things straight, know when you're telling the truth? How do the people who care about you know?"

Claire gaped at him. How much of Bray's memory was back?

The brunette crossed the foyer, saying, "Mrs. Darnell will be right down."

Claire smiled. "Thank you for your help."

She'd met Lily once at Cranesbrook, so she was certain the blonde would recognize her. Now whether Lily would question them as to why she was with Bray was a reason to worry.

"You can have a seat, if you wish." The brunette indicated the couches and armchairs surrounding the fireplace. "Or take a tour of our gift shop."

"Thanks, but we'll wait on the porch," Bray said. "Test out those rockers."

"Fine. I'll send Mrs. Darnell to the veranda, then."

Bray placed a hand at the small of Claire's back and guided her outside. If he knew she was lying about them, why didn't he just say so and get it over with? She felt every finger imprinted into her flesh and wondered if this crazy, stomach-knotting feeling when he touched her would end soon.

Another reason to keep the charade going just a little longer…

THEY BARELY HAD A CHANCE to claim rockers at the end of the veranda before Lily came rushing out the front door, chin-length blond hair swinging around her delicate features, yellow slacks and cotton pullover sweater complementing her pale coloring.

"Bray, thank God you're alive," Lily said, looking from him to Claire.

Claire was doing it again, Bray thought. Touching his arm intimately, like she was staking her claim on him.

Was she?

"Where have you been?" Lily asked. "We thought maybe you were dead and then when the story about the boat blowing up hit the news, Gage went looking for you."

"He went back to St. Stephens?"

Lily nodded. "A couple of hours ago. You might have passed him on the road."

"Maybe you should call him," Claire suggested.

A sound of frustration escaped Lily. "I would, but I found his cell phone on the floor next to the nightstand. There's no way to contact him. I just have to hope he calls me sometime soon, though this place seems to be out of our service area, so he'll have to call the front desk."

They took rockers at the end of the veranda and Bray quickly brought Lily up to speed on what had happened to him and where he'd been and the fact that he, too, had gained a mental power, though one very different from Gage's or Vanderhoven's. He also told her about the supposed evidence they had against him in the altered DVD.

Claire just listened and kept her own counsel, no doubt worried that Lily was going to say something about their being together. Lily kept giving Claire questioning looks as she listened, but apparently she chose to be discreet about Claire's presence.

"I wanted to tell Gage all this in person," Bray said. "I can't even imagine what he's been thinking about me."

"I'll be honest, Bray. He didn't know what to think. He wanted to believe you were innocent, of course, but you know how pragmatic he is. The authorities were convinced you had something to do with the lab accident itself, especially when your niece was kidnapped and you were the ransom. We learned you were having some financial difficulties and—"

"Gage thought someone paid me off to do their dirty work."

Lily shrugged and Claire said, "Bray would never take a bribe."

But she didn't really know if he would or not. Did she have that much trust in him? Or was she simply lying. He couldn't be sure which.

"Gage had some doubts," Lily went on, "but he never gave up on you, Bray. And then when the authorities had you in their radar for the boat explosion, as well, he knew he had to get involved. I guess it's a good thing he forced me to stay behind so someone would be here, or the two of you would be running around in circles, never finding each other."

So what now? Bray wondered. How long before Gage called in so they could set up a rendezvous?

"I was hoping Gage and I could work together like in the old days," he told Lily. "Do a little commando raid on Cranesbrook tonight. If I can find the right objects to touch…"

"You'll finally get some answers," Lily finished for him.

When Bray's cell rang, he said, "That has to be Echo. No one else has this number." He flipped the phone open and said, "What's up?"

"Hey, Bray. Gage was just here."

"Of course." He shook his head at the irony. "We're in Rehoboth Beach with Lily. She said we must have passed Gage on the road."

"Well, at least you have enough time to get back."

"For what?"

"He wants you to meet him tonight at eight at the old lighthouse at Lansdale Point. Do you remember it?"

"Not really, but I'll find it. Landsdale lighthouse at eight. I'll be there. Everything else all right?"

"Zoe and I are fine. And I talked to Rand…um, actually I yelled at him for being such a big jerk with that stunt he pulled. I told him about the DVD, how Claire had figured out it had been faked. Rand really is on our side, Bray."

"You don't know that, Echo."

His sister had been too trusting with men, the reason she'd been left high and dry with a baby. Not that he was going to get into that with her, at least not in front of Claire and Lily, both of whom seemed to be glued to his every word.

"Rand is different, Bray," Echo said. "And I'm in love with him. He saved Zoe. You *have* to like him."

"I can try. Maybe when this is all over."

"No, now. I'm going to tell him about the lighthouse."

"Don't!" No matter what his sister felt for this detective, Bray didn't trust him to work in his best interests. "I'm serious, Echo. I don't want McClellan to interfere with whatever Gage and I plan. We'll handle whatever needs to be handled, like in the military."

He could hear his sister's disappointment.

"Promise you'll call after you and Gage decide on a plan."

He noticed she hadn't agreed to anything. "I'll call."

"Zoe and I love you, Bray. Stay safe."

"I'll be okay. You sit tight and take care of that niece of mine."

Echo made a little noise like a stifled sob. Bray clenched his jaw and hung up on her.

No sooner had he stuffed the cell in his pocket than Claire asked, "What's going on?"

She looked worried. For him? Or for herself?

"Gage stopped at Echo's place, hoping I would be there. Said he had a lead and I should meet him tonight."

"A lead," Lily repeated. "Did he say what?"

Bray shook his head. "But maybe he'll have some ideas by the time Claire and I meet him."

"I'm going with you," Lily said, standing when he did.

"You're going to stay here the way your husband wanted you to," Bray countered. "Gage was concerned for your safety and so am I."

"It's *his* safety I'm worried about." Lily's forehead pulled into a frown. "And yours."

"He and I will be all right. We're trained to watch each other's backs. He loves you and would put you first. You would be a distraction, Lily, you know that. If Gage had you to worry about, he might get sloppy. Not to mention hurt."

He wouldn't say "dead." Too many were dead already. He didn't want to think there might be more.

Bray looked at Claire. "Actually, it wouldn't be a bad idea for you to stay here with Lily."

"I don't think so."

"You wanted that bed and all."

"They're full up."

"There are other bed and breakfasts. We can find you a room."

"You're not leaving me behind," Claire said, her expression mulish.

"I'm not taking you with me."

"You don't have a choice. It's my vehicle. And we're wasting time with this argument, when we could be back on the road. I need time to get something professional-looking to wear if I'm going to get back into Cranesbrook tonight."

Bray didn't continue to argue the case, but he didn't want Claire to get back into Cranesbrook. He'd put her in too much danger already just being with her. He hadn't forgotten how close a call the boat had been. She didn't know enough to make her a threat on her own.

"Lily, if Gage calls, let him know I'll meet him at the lighthouse tonight as requested."

"Will do."

Claire waited until they got to the street before saying, "I'm going, Bray. I'm part of this. I won't be left behind."

But she would be.

If something happened to her, his own life wouldn't be worth saving.

HE'D BEEN SAVING the gun for a special occasion…and this occasion was special enough to make him crack open the wall safe where he'd been keeping the weapon.

After the "accident," he'd taken it from the security chief's office as insurance. Brayden Sloane's fingerprints were all over the piece.

That was why he was wearing gloves.

He would prefer a different method. Something more creative.

What good was his power if he couldn't expand it?

But this particular plan was meant to get rid of the major obstacle that still stood in his way. Gage Darnell would have to surface sometime, and when he did, he, too, would have to be handled.

Then he wouldn't have to resort to such primitive means.

He sat back in his office chair for a moment and turned the gun over, trying to extract from the steel that sense of power men sought. His own power came from within. The thing in his hands was merely a means to an end. Once used, it would be useless to him. He would be done with it.

Once his mistake was erased, he could get on with reshaping his future. No more being a small cog in the giant wheel of life. No more answering to some know-nothing whose title gave him a false sense of power.

He would have *real* power.

He would be a god.

Chapter Fifteen

The tension that tied Claire's stomach in a knot never subsided as they drove west toward St. Stephens. She supposed she ought to be flattered that Bray wanted to keep her safe in the same way Gage did for Lily. Only she wasn't. She might lie to other people, but she never lied to herself. Not purposely, anyway. She knew it wasn't that Bray cared so much for her. She was simply an inconvenience.

Bray was regaining his memory in leaps and bounds, and he was no longer dependent on her. In a few hours, he would have Gage to watch his back.

She already felt Bray's loss.

"I don't know about you, but I'm starving," she complained. "I could use some fuel in addition to a new outfit. Easton is just ahead."

"You're driving. It's your vehicle."

"Is that why you've been sulking?"

"I haven't been sulking. I've been thinking."

About her? Claire decided not to flatter herself. Of course Bray had been thinking about what answers tonight might bring.

"Are you familiar with Lansdale Point?" he asked.

"Sorry. Never been there. But once we get to Easton, I can look it up on the Internet."

"You think we'll find an Internet café?"

"Don't need to. I'll hack into a signal."

"So you're good at hacking?"

"I know a few things."

"Then why haven't you been able to get into the Project Cypress files?"

"It's not been for a lack of trying." She explained her failed methodology of using the key logger program and her conclusion that the password had to be obtained using a physical key. "If only I could find it, I could get us some answers." She realized her solution might be sitting next to her. "Wait a minute. *You* could find the key."

"How so?"

"You could be a human key logger," Claire said. "All you have to do is touch the computers used by the project team members and see what comes to you. Maybe we'll luck out and you'll see one of the scientists logging in."

"But the password would be encrypted."

"It's not the password I'm after. Even if you could see the number, you probably wouldn't be able to duplicate it, because it's bound to be hundreds or even thousands of numerals long. But you might be able to help locate one of the SDs—Secure Digital chips. Using that, I can get in."

"Or Gage can. He's pretty slick with computers."

He was trying to push her out again, as if she wasn't part of this. "Computers aren't his life," she said smoothly. "They're mine."

Sad to say, it was true, and one of the reasons she'd applied for the job at Cranesbrook in the first place. Her mother had recently moved to Florida with her latest lover, and her brother lived in Minneapolis, her sister in L.A. That left her with a lot of people who were more like good acquaintances than close friends. She'd figured if she got the job at Cranesbrook, at least she would be living close to the one person she could always count on, her best friend, Mac.

The reminder had her glancing at her hand with the class ring, remembering how corny Mac had been when he'd given it to her. *Now we're officially going steady,* he'd teased. Even then she'd realized the limitations of their relationship. Romantically he preferred someone with broader shoulders and a little beard stubble. At that time, he'd needed a cover and she'd been happy telling one more lie to protect him.

Her coming up with a plan seemed to mellow Bray out. Rather than sitting next to her like a stone, he actually talked to her as if he cared. The good will continued through a fast dinner at a small café decorated in second-hand chic. While they ate, Claire easily picked up a wireless signal and got directions to the lighthouse.

Then afterward, when Bray headed for the men's room, she retrieved her e-mail just in case something important awaited her. Spam filter or not, some junk got through anyway. There were a few e-mails from friends, one from her sister.

And one from Mac.

Claire's pulse surged and she stared at his name for a moment before looking at the date. It had been sent that very day.

As she opened the email, Claire felt the pressure in her chest magnify.

C—
Get out now while you still can.
M

Her heart began to thunder. The pressure in her chest amplified. Mac had always used their initials rather than full names in his e-mail messages to her. The addy was his. And he'd replied to one of the dozens of e-mails she'd sent to him right after he'd disappeared.

Mac Ellroy was alive!

After all this time, he'd finally answered her pleas for communication.

Why now? And why so cryptic?

Why hadn't he told her what had happened to him or how to contact him?

Most of all, how had he known she could be in trouble?

Did he still have some connection to Cranesbrook? How long ago had he learned she'd taken the job? Had he figured out she'd been trying to hack into Project Cypress files?

Her mind whirled with questions.

She tapped out a rapid reply asking him how she could find him. Then she stared at the screen, willing him to be right there online, willing him to answer her.

Nothing.

So she tapped out another message—this one asking him to tell her anything he could about Project Cypress. She admitted that she knew her investigating was dangerous and that she'd learned there'd been a big cover-up, including an exchange of funds and murder.

Even as she hit Send, Bray returned to the table.

"I'll get the bill," he said, seeming not to notice her palpable tension. "Let's get on the road so we can get you that change of clothes you want and still get to the lighthouse by eight."

"Sure, it'll just take me a minute to close down."

And to calm down.

Claire used the time it took Bray to settle the bill to breathe and steady herself as she waited a moment to see if she would get a reply from Mac. Nothing. She shut down her system. Somehow she got herself together. Somehow by the time she caught up to Bray at the entrance to the restaurant, she was wearing her game face.

Mac was alive. Thank God. Not that it altered her own situation. She still had to know what had happened, what had made him disappear. She still had to help Bray clear his name, and maybe Mac, as well. She still had to help bring an end to the cover-up that had resulted in lost lives.

That Mac might be part of it occurred to Claire, but she forced the unthinkable away.

Not Mac.

She knew him too well to think he would do something underhanded.

As they left the restaurant, Bray asked, "What's the deal with buying new clothes anyway? You look fine."

She'd added a hoodie to her jogging pants and top. Not exactly haute couture.

"For an excursion to a beach and lighthouse, this is suitable. But once we hook up with Gage, I'm assuming we're going to head for Cranesbrook. I need to look as professional as employees there are used to seeing. You don't want me to raise any flags."

"Fine."

Bray didn't argue, and Claire thought he was probably humoring her.

They stopped at the first store they came to on a main street, and Bray made her buy the first pantsuit that fit her. Borrowing a pair of scissors from the clerk, she removed all tags. Thankfully, her shoes in the CRV would still do. She didn't think Bray's good will would hold up for another stop to shop. Not knowing what the lighthouse area would be like, she threw the bag of clothing in the back of the vehicle. She could change clothes later.

Then they were on their way, traveling fast toward the lighthouse and what probably would be the end of their relationship.

So FAR, HIS MISSION had been a bust.

A frustrated Gage Darnell stood in the middle of Bray's deserted house. He'd used his telekinesis to get in and now wished it were in his power to conjure up his ex-partner.

Trying to track Bray down had proven to be a waste of time. None of the employees at the marina could give him any information. No one there even knew Bray other than one of the cafe's waitresses, and she'd only seen him once and briefly the morning before.

Next he'd hit Bray's usual haunts—the places they'd gone to eat or drink on the many occasions Bray had pulled him from the Baltimore office for a meeting. But no, Bray hadn't been around since the accident.

Finally he'd come here to Bray's home and had practically ransacked the place looking for some kind of clue. Futile, he'd known even as he'd searched, because someone—the Feds, no doubt—had preceded him.

Still, he'd had to try.

It was now clear that Bray was alive and that he'd been connected to another explosion. Gage had felt it his duty to find his partner and make him talk.

For the past two weeks he'd wavered between wanting to believe in Bray's innocence and fearing the man he thought he knew was guilty of messing up over a fat payday. He still didn't know which was true. He only knew he wanted his partner to be innocent, hoped to hell that Bray hadn't betrayed his country for thirty pieces of silver.

Not knowing where to check next, Gage decided to call Echo. She hadn't answered earlier, but this time she picked up after the first ring.

"It's Gage," he said.

"What's going on? Did that lead pan out?"

"What lead?"

"When you left here, you said you had a lead to follow up."

"When I left it was for some one-on-one time with Lily."

"You saw Lily this afternoon?"

"This morning before I left Rehoboth Beach." Silence. Gage frowned. What the hell was going on? "Is Bray there?" Is that why she was sounding so odd.

"No. I haven't seen my brother since this morning. But I called him this afternoon and told him to meet you like you said." Echo paused. "You sound like you don't know what I'm talking about."

"Because I don't."

"You came to my place this afternoon and—"

"No, I didn't."

Silence again. Gage's mind was whirling. What the heck was going on? Did he have a look-alike? Surely, Echo would be able to tell the difference between them. Unless…

His hackles rose.

"Echo, I'm serious. I wasn't at your place. I've been trying to track Bray down for hours. I've been to the marina, bars, restaurants. Not to your place."

"But I saw you. Spoke to you. Are you sure you don't have some kind of amnesia like Bray has?"

"Amnesia." That explained why his partner had done that disappearing act. *If* the amnesia was for real. It didn't explain why Echo thought he'd paid her a visit. "Let's start from the beginning. Tell me what we talked about."

Gage listened with a growing sense of alarm, especially when Echo got to the part about Bray's getting other peoples' memories through touching objects. He hadn't been the one parked on Echo's doorstep earlier receiving that intel. That alone was cause for suspicion. But beyond that, Pseudo-Gage hadn't gone inside. He'd stayed in the doorway as though he *couldn't* go in…as though he were some sort of projection that couldn't leave his creator's line of sight.

Why not? Each person who'd breathed in the chemicals had had a different reaction. Had gained a different mental power. Telekinesis, augmenting emotions, picking up memories…so why not projection?

When Echo got to the part about the meeting at the lighthouse, he checked his watch.

"Gage, do you remember any of this?"

"I wasn't at your place today, Echo." Seventeen minutes to eight. Not much time to get there. "Someone else made you think I was here. Someone who got a different power from those chemicals than the rest of us did. Someone is setting Bray up."

Echo gasped. "What are we going to do?"

"Hang in there, okay? I'm on my way to the lighthouse now."

BRAY FIGURED the switch would come at the lighthouse. They'd meet Gage there, then he would let Gage drive and send Claire on her way to someplace safe. The question was how. Getting her to back off wasn't going to be easy. She was the most stubborn woman he'd ever met.

Well, at least the most stubborn he could remember.

According to the Internet, Lansdale Point was about a fifteen-minute drive northwest of town. The car clock read 7:48. And they were almost there.

"So, anything coming to you about the significance of this lighthouse?" she asked.

"Not a thing, but Gage must have a good reason to want to meet out there. Privacy, for one."

The road was deserted and twisted along the coast. The lighthouse probably marked shoals, a dangerous area for boats to get through. He could see glimpses of water, but the moon kept tucking itself under a cloud cover, so other than what was on the road in front of them, they were driving blind.

"I suppose you're right about the privacy," Claire said. "Though I would think Gage could have suggested someplace a little more convenient. Maybe he needs to show you something connected to Cranesbrook at that location."

Although Bray couldn't imagine what. Damn his memory!

Or maybe not.

If he'd had his memory, he might never have gotten together with Claire. She wouldn't have been able to trick him. He never would have spent all this time with her.

He never would have put her in danger.

Though he thought she might have done that to herself anyway, he couldn't help but feel responsible for her. Liar or not, she was a human being, one who roused unfamiliar feelings in him. If anything happened to her, he couldn't live with himself. If she was too close, worry would distract him and he needed as clear a head as he could manage. He had to find a way to make her back off.

The vehicle was slowing and the area ahead lit for a second. The lighthouse.

"You can pull up over there," Bray, said, pointing.

"I think I'll go a little farther, find some cover. You know, just in case."

Just in case there was danger?

Claire would be in danger if she stuck with him through the night. How to make her run in the other direction was the question. Then it came to him—a way he could put a safe enough distance between them.

"Tell me something, Claire," he said as she pulled

into an area protected by some wild-looking shrubs and trees. "Why'd you get yourself involved in this whole Cranesbrook mess?"

"Because of you, of course."

"The real reason."

"Real? Aren't you real enough?" she asked, a slight tightness in her voice giving her away as she stopped the vehicle.

"But surely there's something more."

"It isn't enough that I'm trying to help my husband clear his name?" When he chose not to answer, she sighed. "Okay, I also don't like people disappearing and getting killed or kidnapped."

"But you're not a cop. Right?"

"You know I'm not."

"I only know for sure what you tell me."

"Well, I'm not a cop."

"And you're not working for the other team?"

"Other team? What are you intimating, Bray? What other team?"

Though she was trying to repress her anger, it seeped through her words, which came as something of a relief to Bray. If she were guilty of being a switch-hitter, he might hear caution in her tone. Or bravado. But not anger.

"You tell me, Claire."

"This is a weird conversation. Can we drop it?"

"Because you're uncomfortable? I don't think so. Not when it's just getting interesting."

"If you don't trust me, just say so."

"*Should* I trust you?"

"Yes!"

Here it came. "Then stop lying to me."

Claire didn't even try to deny it. She simply went silent. Bray willed her to tell him the truth. The *whole* truth.

So when she said, "I don't know what you want me to say," he finally spoke his mind.

"I want you to start being honest with me. Or is that too much to ask? I've given you every opportunity to come clean." He paused, gave her yet another chance. Nothing, so he went on. "I know we're not married, Claire. I know you're nothing to me." That wasn't true—she was quickly becoming his everything—but he said it with conviction so she would believe it. "So why? What did you think you'd get out of this charade? What was your motivation? Mac Ellroy—this lab tech who disappeared—did you love him?"

She didn't even hesitate before saying, "Yes!"

There it was. The thing Bray had been most afraid of. Well, not most. She could have been a traitor or she could have gotten herself killed, either of which would have been worse. Still, he couldn't help but feel his gut twist at the acknowledgment.

Whatever he felt for her didn't matter in the long run. As soon as she got the answers she wanted, she would be gone, just like his old man.

"You're really good at this," he said, wondering if she felt anything at all for him. Even if she said so, how could he believe it? Lies came too easily to her. She'd stuck to him like glue because she thought he held all the answers locked in his chemically altered brain. "You'll go to any lengths to get what you want."

"Bray, please—"

He interrupted. "You even slept with me, Claire." He had her on the hook and he wasn't about to let go until he was certain he could make her turn her back on him for her own protection. Even so, he felt like the dirt under his shoe when he said, "Your being so easy doesn't paint a very pretty picture of you."

Claire gasped and Bray got out of the vehicle before he could soften and admit he didn't mean that.

Hopefully, he'd been cruel enough to drive her away from him and the danger he would face that night.

As he headed for the lighthouse, Bray realized that to protect Claire, he'd just lied to her twice.

The lighthouse at Lansdale Point was squat, octagonal and set on stilts. It was a screw-pile lighthouse suspended above water by cast-iron pilings with corkscrew-like bases driven into the sea floor. Bray could see its red-and-white facade every time the brilliant beam at the peak blipped. A ramp led from the lighthouse over several yards of water to a sandy area.

Considering the tide was coming in fast, he wondered how long the entry to the ramp would stay on dry ground. The structure itself was dark inside, whether closed for the season or for good, he couldn't tell.

Not seeing Gage's Jeep anywhere, he headed straight for the ramp.

The night was dark. While a nearly full moon hung in the sky, a bank of clouds hid it. Rain was imminent.

No doubt the rains wouldn't be pleasant. Hopefully, the weather would hold till the wee hours of the morning.

In the meantime, the wind blew in gusts and little

whirls of sand lifted from the beach floor. The stronger the gust, the more the sand stung.

Bray had an itchy feeling at the back of his neck that had nothing to do with the sand. Something was off, not quite right, though he couldn't nail it. It didn't help that the way the lighthouse beam flashed gave the area a macabre feel. He glanced back once to see that Claire hadn't moved. She'd neither followed him, nor had she left the area. Her vehicle sat there, lights on, her engine's hum the only sound competing with the water lapping at the shore.

His gut twisted at how his lies must have made her feel. He'd done it for her own good, to keep her safe, so why didn't she drive away?

He almost went back. Almost followed his impulse to apologize, to tell her what he'd said wasn't true. In the end, he steeled himself against those softer feelings and pushed against the wind toward the lighthouse.

CLAIRE FINALLY SHUT OFF the engine, stuffed her Maglite in her pocket, left the vehicle and headed after Bray. She was part of this. Her life had been at risk. And despite Bray's insult added to the warning from Mac, she wasn't running the other way.

The wind had picked up and a chill shot down her back. She pulled up her hoodie and jogged to stay warm, first on solid ground, then across the sand. A spray of water hit her face and she realized the sky was spritzing. She could see Bray ahead, a dark silhouette against the darker night, but there was no sign of anyone else, and she wondered why Gage would use subterfuge in such a secluded area. Something didn't feel right. Instincts humming, she moved faster.

"Bray, wait for me!"

The beam flashed and she saw him glance back, then simply forge up the ramp to the deck surrounding the squat structure. Claire cursed and kept going. A moment later she was racing upward, gasping for breath.

"Bray, where are you?" she called in a stage whisper, though she didn't know why since they seemed to be the only ones out here.

"Right here," he said from directly behind her.

Whipping around brought her practically against his chest. The lighthouse beam blipped, illuminating his closed expression. Angry or not, she couldn't help but respond physically to him. She wanted to press herself against his body and wrap her arms around his neck. Suspecting he would no longer appreciate the gesture, she took a step back.

"What are you doing here, Claire?"

"The same as you." She moved away from him and began circling the deck that surrounded the lighthouse. "Waiting for Gage to show up."

"Get out now, while you can."

The words were almost identical to those in Mac's message.

"I don't want out. I want answers."

"You could get a hell of a lot more trouble than you bargained for."

"What's life without a little risk?"

His fingers wrapped around her arm and jerked her to a stop. "Are you really that naive or is this part of your act?"

"Forget it. You're not driving me away no matter what you say."

Claire realized that had been his purpose in saying those awful things to her. He'd wanted her out of the way. Not that it made her feel any better.

She jerked her arm out of Bray's grasp and whirled away from him. She hadn't taken more than two steps before her foot caught in something soft. The beam blipped and she grabbed on to the railing and reached down to the obstacle. Cloth gave way to cool flesh. Her gorge rose in her throat when she realized she was up close and personal with a body.

"What happened?" Bray demanded. "Are you all right?"

"I'm okay, but he's not. I think I just found Gage."

Chapter Sixteen

Lily Darnell felt as if she'd paced the floor between her four poster bed and the seating area in front of the fireplace until the carpet in between was nearly worn.

Why hadn't Gage called her?

How could he have forgotten his cell phone?

Seething with frustration, she felt her head go light when her own cell phone finally rang. With fumbling fingers, she pulled it from her pocket, but rather than Bray, the call was from Echo.

"I wasn't going to call you, and then I thought if it was me and Rand, I would want to know."

"Know what?" Knees trembling, Lily perched on the edge of the bed and stared out the window that looked over the water. Too dark now to see anything.

"I told Bray that Gage wanted to meet him at Lansdale lighthouse, but it wasn't really Gage."

Lily grew cold as she listened to Echo's tale about the two Gages and about how the real Gage figured Bray was in trouble and was hell-bent on saving him.

"I just thought you ought to know."

"You warned Bray, right?"

"No signal. And he has a pre-pay cell—no voice mail. I left a message for Rand, but he hasn't gotten back to me. I feel so helpless. I don't know what to do."

"I need to find a car," Lily said. If she stayed in Rehoboth Beach, she would feel equally helpless. "I wonder if I can get a rental this late. I need to get back to St. Stephens. Call me the instant you hear anything."

"Sure. Lily, I'm really sorry."

"There's nothing to be sorry for. Not for either of us. Gage and Bray are going to be okay."

Lily kept telling herself that as she grabbed a wallet out of her purse and rushed downstairs only to be told the rental agencies were closed for the night.

"It's an emergency," she said. "I have to get back to St. Stephens right away. I'll pay anything. Please, it's my husband."

In the end, the brunette softened and called a friend who worked at one of the car rental places. Soon Lily would be on her way back to St. Stephens without a clue as to what she would do when she arrived there.

WHEN CLAIRE SNAPPED on her Maglite and swept it along the body sprawled back on the deck, the first thing Bray saw was the bloom of red covering the victim's white lab coat right where his heart would be.

Bray let out his breath. "That's not Gage."

"No, it's Hank Riddell." She reached out and felt for a pulse, then looked up at Bray, her face shadowed by the hood of her jogging suit. "He's dead."

"What's that next to him?"

Claire focused the light on the weapon next to the body.

"Don't touch it," Bray warned her. "Fingerprints."

And his would probably be all over the damn thing. He was pretty certain it was the gun he'd kept in the Cranesbrook security office. With each passing hour, he was remembering more and more. Kind of like a megafile being loaded into a computer, slowly, one frustrating bite at a time.

"Is this what Gage wanted me to see?" he asked.

"Why isn't he here, then?"

Water lapped against the piles below them. Bray was tempted to throw the damn gun as far as he could into the water, but of course he couldn't destroy evidence, not even if it pointed to him.

Before he could decide on a course of action, a bright beam came at him, followed by a deep voice. "Freeze right there, Sloane."

Bray whirled around to see dark uniforms behind twin flashlights tromping up the ramp. Police uniforms. What the hell! Had he been set up by his own partner?

One of the cops got on his radio and called in. "Yep, Sloane's here just like the anonymous tip said. And there's another body. Guy in a lab coat. Must be from Cranesbrook. Send an ambulance to pick him up."

A siren announced the arrival of another police car. Backup had already arrived. The light flashed and he could see the car pulling in at the opposite side of the point from Claire's CRV. Silently cursing Gage, Bray began to sweat. He couldn't be taken in. Not when he was so close to answers. And now Claire would be implicated unless he got her out of here before the cops got a good look at her face. Thankfully, the hood was still hiding her identity.

"Over here!" one of the cops yelled to the new arrivals.

"The victim's name is Hank Riddell," Bray said. "Look, we just got here and found him like that."

"You'll get a chance to give your side of the story at the station."

Another siren. One of the cops glanced back and Bray saw his chance. He jammed a shoulder into the other officer as he lunged toward the water side, grabbing Claire and jerking her into following. They hit the railing and scrambled over it together. Then they were falling and crashing feet-first into the cold water. Luckily the tide was in. Bray hit the bottom with a jerk.

The lighthouse beam flashed, allowing him to see that Claire was right next to him. He put his finger to his lips as quick footsteps tattooed against the ramp.

"Shit, we gotta go in after them?"

"Nah, they have to come out somewhere," one of the new arrivals said. "Too cold to stay in long. All we have to do is stay put and wait."

Bray held on to Claire and lifted his feet from the sea bottom. The flesh under his fingers trembled and he realized how cold she was. He pulled her closer to conserve body heat. She went stiff but didn't fight him. The current was taking them downstream away from the cops and toward the area where she'd parked her car.

"Hey, I see movement over that way!" someone shouted. "Don't let 'em get away."

The beam blipped and Bray saw the cops run in the opposite direction. All but one guy who backed away from the others and signaled them.

Gage Darnell!

What the hell was going on?

By the next blip, Gage had moved far enough back from the water line to be hidden by shrubs and tall beach grasses. He was waving frantically for them to come in. Bray realized he'd sent the cops on a wild-goose chase.

Splatters of rain hit the water around them. Claire was now shaking against him from the cold. He held her tight and began moving toward shore, one eye on the activity down the beach, the other on his partner, who'd sent the cops off in the wrong direction. Could he trust Gage? It couldn't be a mere coincidence that his partner had wanted to meet here and then Riddell turned up dead.

"Stay low," he told Claire as they hit shallow water.

They crept onto land half bent over. The lighthouse beam flashed, revealing a Jeep next to the CRV. Gage was already there. By the time they caught up to him, the rain was starting to come down in fits and starts.

"Claire, I'm going with Gage."

"Then so am I."

"No. I don't want you with us in case the cops catch us." Or in case Gage betrayed them. He still didn't know what to think about his partner, but Bray wasn't letting Gage out of his sight until he knew what was what. "They couldn't see your face with that hood up, so they don't know who you are."

"He's right, Claire," Gage said. "I'll drive past them so they'll come after us. That'll give you a chance to get away. Head west and keep your lights off as long as you can."

Claire shook her head.

"Do it!" Bray said, opening her driver's door and pushing her to get inside. He held her arm a moment longer than necessary, knowing it might be the last time he would ever touch her.

She pulled her arm from his gasp and slammed the door in his face.

By the time Bray climbed into the Jeep, Gage was already in the driver's seat. "Let's get going. We have a lot to talk about."

"We have some cops to lose first." Gage started the engine.

Bray looked out the window as the beam blipped. Claire's hood was off and she was wiping her eyes. Sea water? Or was she crying? He swallowed his guilt as Gage pulled out and swung past the official vehicles. He heard a shout and saw flashlight beams bob toward them as the officers ran for their vehicles in the now driving rain.

Gage drove like a madman. But then he always had, the reason Bray had let him have command of the Humvee in Afghanistan. As they whipped around curves and turns, Bray felt his brain jar into motion, speeding up the memories about the night of the lab accident until there was only one thing missing. The aftermath of the explosion.

"Head for Cranesbrook."

"As soon as I'm sure I've lost them."

Gage circled around their objective. The rain let up and Bray saw a pair of lights in the distance behind them.

"I think they got us."

"Not yet."

Gage drove straight off the road and down into a ravine where he cut his lights and the engine. A minute later the other set of lights sailed right past.

"So what the hell is going on, Gage? Why did you get me to come to a murder scene?"

"You were set up, but not by me. I'm not the one who paid your sister a visit this afternoon. I believe we've got a fourth person who inhaled the chemicals. One with a new power."

Gage filled him in on his assumption that a fourth person's brain had mutated, enabling him to project an image that made Echo believe she'd been speaking to Gage.

"A fourth person came into the lab?" Bray was still trying to fill that hole in his memory.

"As far as I know, the only people affected by the accident were Vanderhoven, me and you."

"What if the fourth guy wasn't a part of the accident? What if one of our intrepid scientists decided to experiment on himself?"

"You mean, inhale the chemicals purposely?"

"Claire found some vials and what sounds like a flashpot in a storeroom in what supposedly was an empty lab. A janitor died in there."

"You mean, Artur? I heard he'd died of a heart attack."

"But caused by what? Claire said Riddell found him. And now Riddell's dead. Murdered."

"It's all tied together, everything that's happened since the accident."

"We came to the same conclusion."

We... He and Claire. He already missed her. He

wanted to believe there was some way they could be together again, but he simply didn't see how when their short relationship had been nothing but a lie. He needed to focus on what they were doing. Even thinking about Claire was too distracting.

"Can I use your cell?" he asked Gage. "Mine took a swim and I need to let Echo know I'm okay."

"Yeah, sure." Gage pulled it from his jacket pocket and handed it to Bray. "And I have some dry sweats in the back that should fit you." He paused a second while Bray tapped out his sister's number, then said, "She'll corroborate my story."

Bray didn't protest. And indeed, when Echo got on the phone, she did exactly that. Relief shot through Bray and he finally relaxed. When Echo asked him what they were going to do next, he gave her the truth, including the fact that the police arrived right after they found Riddell, ending with, "We're going to break into Cranesbrook and do what's necessary to get some answers."

Something told him that the mastermind behind the cover-up and all the deaths would be waiting for them.

GREAT SOBS RACKED Claire for all of a minute before anger won over heartbreak. If Bray really thought she could be sent packing so easily, he had another think coming. She had as much at stake as he did, now being the target of both a murderer and a police investigation.

The muffled sound of sirens intruded, but soon they faded. So the chase was on. Shedding the wet hoodie and throwing it in back, she started her engine, slid out of her parking spot and coasted in the other direction, all the while checking her rearview mirror. Gradually she picked up speed, turned on her running lights, steeled herself for what she was going to do next.

Halfway to Cranesbrook, she pulled into the parking lot of a diner. Grabbing the bag with the new clothes and finding her umbrella, she stepped out into the rain that had now petered off to a fine drizzle. She entered the diner and looked around. The place was half empty.

"O-oh, darlin', you been swimming?" asked a waitress, who was wielding a pot of coffee at the counter where three customers turned to look at her.

Claire gave them all an abashed grin and took on another persona. "Looks like it, don't it? You'd think a girl would have the sense to take her umbrella when it's fixin' to rain."

"I see you got it now."

"Dry clothes, too. That's why I'm not taking any chances. Do you think you could have a big cup of hot Joe to go by the time I'm out of the ladies' room?"

"Sure enough, darlin'. How do you take it?"

"Straight up'll do."

"You got it."

Claire rushed into the restroom, where she quickly got into dry clothes. That felt better. Then she took her hair down from its clip, finger-combed it and fluffed it in front of the electric hand-dryer.

A glance in the mirror assured her she was now presentable if not glamorous. She grabbed her bag of wet clothes and her umbrella and went to pay for her coffee. Even her money was wet when she took out her wallet.

"Oh, you did go swimming," the waitress said with a laugh.

Claire took a sip from the foam cup. "Ah, that's better." Warmth trickled to her stomach. "You have a good night now."

"Back at ya, darlin'."

Claire left the diner knowing the waitress would remember her. That didn't mean she would cooperate with a cop asking questions about a woman on the run. Besides, the place was far enough away from Lansdale Point that no one would think to search for her here.

Though she raced to the car, umbrella up, she couldn't avoid the rain altogether. Still, she felt about seventy percent better. Taking another sip of hot coffee, starting the engine and turning on the heat increased that percentage. On the outside anyway.

Inside, she was still cold and numb. She and Bray were over, but she would have to deal with those emotions later. Now she had to get to Cranesbrook before all hell let loose.

"YOU'RE SURE this is going to work?"

"Watch and become a believer."

The moon had broken through the cloud bank to cast a cold blue light over the Cranesbrook complex. Bray could see the metal box attached to the nearby building that held landscaping tools and janitorial supplies. The box housed the controls for the electrified fence. Being that Five Star had installed the system, Gage knew exactly what had to be done to cut the electricity so they could get into the complex unharmed and undetected. The power box's door suddenly whipped open. Gage continued to focus his energy on the controls.

Whatever might be happening was a mystery to Bray because he couldn't see inside.

Gage stepped back and said, "Power's off, so let's do this fast," then focused on the fence itself. A section of chain-link started to rattle. "You remember how to walk on your belly?"

"Watch me."

A frisson of excitement zapped through Bray as the chain-link separated itself from one of the posts and curled upward several inches. On the ground on his stomach, he slithered under the fence without so much as brushing it. Then he rolled up onto his feet as Gage followed. They were in!

Quickly, Gage reversed his mental wizardry, fixing and re-electrifying the fence so it would seem to any security guard on his toes as if there simply had been an interruption of power rather than a break-in.

They'd picked a back way onto the property, along a road seldom used. Even then, they'd hidden the Jeep in a little ravine some distance away and had walked back to where they wanted to get in, just to be sure.

Now they kept to the perimeter of the physical plant supply building. Also according to plan, Gage used his mind to manipulate the locked door. They slid inside and found the closet holding extra worker's uniforms. Gage easily climbed into a janitor's jumpsuit, but being bulkier through the shoulders and chest, Bray had to find the biggest one available, and even then it was a tight squeeze. He grabbed two billed caps and handed one to Gage.

"Not much of a disguise, but it'll have to do."

Gage nodded. "We'll get by."

Ransacking the pockets of the jacket he'd worn into the facility, Gage pulled out two Maglites, a role of duct tape and a handful of plastic ties, which he shared with Bray. They both shoved everything into their jumpsuit pockets and then were on the move.

They got within spitting distance of the main building before they saw the guard posted outside the back door.

"What the hell! They didn't have anyone posted when I broke in the other night."

"They didn't know you were alive then."

"So how do we do this without raising the alarm? He's not going to let us get by him without a fight."

"Then we bring him to us."

The next thing Bray knew, the security guard's cap flew toward them, as if a gust of wind had blown it off his head. The guard cursed and scrambled after it, but the cap was on the move. A little pop like a gust of wind flipped it, and then it went spinning. The guard was so focused on retrieving his cap that he didn't see Bray come up behind him until it was too late. Bray already had hold of his carotid artery, applying just enough force so that the man's body was tricked into lowering his blood pressure and knocking him out. The security guard dropped like a sack of potatoes to the ground.

Before the man could regain consciousness, Bray ripped a piece of duct tape and placed it across his mouth so he couldn't call out for backup. Then he turned the guard onto his stomach, pulled his hands behind his back and used a plastic tie as he would handcuffs. By the time he did the same to the man's feet, Gage had opened the rear exit door.

Rushing inside, they stopped dead at the more formidable obstacle in their path.

"Took you long enough to get here."

Claire glared at them both, spun on her heel and led the way down the corridor.

Chapter Seventeen

Striding down the hall toward the offices, Claire played it cool and collected when inside she was a jumble of nerves. Her chest felt too tight and her stomach was a little rocky, but she was never going to let on. A master at this game, she was never going to let Bray know how she felt about him. Or that he'd broken her heart. As far as he was concerned, she was part of the team. She'd been along for the ride to further her investigation. Period.

Having arrived nearly twenty minutes before, she'd been ready to jump out of her skin by the time the rear door had finally opened. Now she could calm down.

You'd think.

"I checked to see who's working late," Claire said far more coolly than she was feeling. "We're in luck. Being that it's a Saturday night, other than the security guards and cleaning crew, no one's working."

Gage asked, "You can be sure of this how?"

"Right from the night-entry guard's mouth. That doesn't mean someone can't change his mind and come into work late, though, so let's do what we have to and fast."

"Where are you taking us?"

"First stop, Hank Riddell's office. Maybe a dead man can tell us a tale."

The research fellow had been assigned one of the inside windowless offices hardly bigger than a coat closet. Shelving surrounded his desk, the only furniture.

"I'm looking for one of two things—either a flash drive or a postage-stamp-size secure digital chip that would be inserted right here." She tapped the slot on his computer with her forefinger. "Have at it."

Gage stood in the doorway, back to them, and Claire figured he was keeping watch. Just in case.

She glanced at Bray, who was touching the USB port but not seeming to get anything out of it.

"Try sitting in his chair and relaxing."

Bray did as she suggested and made another attempt, then slipped his hand up to the SD slot. This time tension seemed to fill him immediately.

"What do you see?"

"He's popping a secure device chip into the slot."

"Nothing to indicate where it came from? A cell phone, digital camera—"

"Phone," Bray interrupted. "Open on the table."

"Which the police probably have now," Claire said with a discouraged sigh. "No doubt he had it on him when he died."

Even so, they took the time to search the office just in case he had a spare. Their effort proved to be in vain.

"Where next?" Gage asked.

"Dr. Ulrich's office. Project Cypress is his baby."

She led them to the executive offices and Ulrich's suite. They went through the same routine.

Bray sighed and shook his head. "His wallet. He keeps his SD in his wallet."

"Great. Unless we find him and roll him, we're out of luck again."

They went through the motions of a search even knowing they would find nothing.

They next tried Kelso's office, but his computer didn't yield any visions that pertained to Project Cypress security.

"I don't get it," Claire said. "Kelso is temporarily in charge of Cranesbrook Associates. And he's in charge of security anyway. He would need access to the files."

"Maybe he doesn't have the interest," Gage said.

Bray added, "Or maybe he's the kind of guy who wants written reports on his desk."

So they searched his desk and his file cabinets for any folders containing Project Cypress information. Gage even used his telekinesis to open a locked cabinet.

Nothing.

"That's it, then," Gage said. "We'll just have to concentrate on the Project Cypress lab itself."

"Which one?" Bray asked.

Claire said, "All of them, if necessary. Lab 7 was the original."

"Been there, done that."

The way he was looking at her, she wasn't sure if he meant the lab…or her.

Trying to block out the personal feelings he was stirring up, Claire focused on Gage. "The project was then moved to Lab 3. But those vials of chemicals I found—those were in the Lab 12 storeroom."

"That was yesterday," Bray reminded her. "The stuff could've been moved."

"Or maybe not," Gage said. "No harm in covering as much territory as we can. What about the security guard at the front desk, though? He'll be able to see our every move on the lab cameras."

"Not if he isn't awake to do so," Bray said. "And turn off the damn system while you're at it. Amazing things they can do with security DVDs these days."

"You can manage without hurting him, right?" Claire asked Gage.

"Yes, ma'am. And which lab are you and Bray headed for?"

"Before we go anywhere, I want to try one more office."

Bray frowned. "There's someone else involved with Project Cypress?"

"There was. Sid Edmonston."

"Edmonston's dead," Gage protested.

"But he had access to everything."

"A waste of time." Gage shook his head. "The authorities have been through his office more than once. Local. State. Feds. If there was a cell phone or a digital camera in there, it's long gone, taken as evidence."

"I'm just trying to be thorough."

Gage was already on the move. "I'll meet you when I have the security guard situation in hand."

"Don't hurt him," Claire called after Gage.

"He's not going to hurt someone who's innocent," Bray said.

"How can you be sure?"

"Because I know him."

And now Bray knew her. It seemed his memory was back in fighting form. Why couldn't he have remembered something helpful from the get-go? Maybe then she wouldn't have gotten so emotionally tangled up with him.

"We gave you a clean getaway," he said. "Why did you come back?"

Whatever he was feeling about them wasn't evident unless it was irritation. Or maybe that was due to his having to baby-sit her. Well, too bad.

"I'm part of this," Claire said, moving out of Kelso's office. "Someone I care for deeply is involved."

"Involved? You said Mac Ellroy disappeared."

She hadn't been thinking of Mac, though she should have been. "He did. Then I got an e-mail from him today."

"So you're off the hook."

Entering Edmonston's office suite, she said, "Mac didn't answer any of my questions, and I don't have a clue as to where to find him. He simply told me to get out while I still can."

"Good advice."

Unable to keep the irony from her tone, Claire said, "You sound like you care."

She waited in vain for Bray to respond. Instead of connecting with her, he went straight into the late president's office and sat at the computer. She let out the breath she'd been holding and followed. Bray was just turning on the system that had been shut down since Edmonston's death.

"So this Mac—did you ever consider he might be part of the problem?"

"No." At least not seriously, though she had wondered if Mac had gotten himself into something he couldn't get out of.

"Maybe you don't know him as well as you think you do."

"I know that he would do anything for me, even put himself between me and Mom's boyfriend, who had about thirty pounds on him and a nasty attitude."

"What? You lied to your mom's boyfriend and got him hot under the collar?"

"Would that be a good enough excuse for him to try to rape his lover's sixteen-year-old daughter?"

Bray stared at her and Claire wished she could take back the horrible truth she'd never told anyone before. Well, she'd tried to tell her mom, but the woman had refused to believe her and had even suggested that it was all a lie meant to break them up because Claire was jealous of her. Swallowing hard, she tore her gaze from Bray's and glanced at the monitor.

"The system is up."

Her words registered on Bray and he turned to the computer. The moment he touched the CPU, his expression grew intent. His concentration seemed absolute, as if he were in the midst of one of his visions. Seeming dazed, he looked around the office as if he were searching for something specific.

"What?" Claire asked.

Rather than answer, Bray rose from the desk and crossed to the credenza, stopping in front of the iPod docked in a digital sound system. Claire's pulse rushed.

"Is that it?" she asked.

He picked the iPod from the dock, his forehead

pulling as he concentrated. "I believe it is." He held it out to her.

Their fingers brushed and a thrill shot through her as she quickly took the device from him and opened the back. Picking out the SD, she sat in front of the computer. Bray leaned in close to watch as she popped the postage-stamp-size chip into the slot. Too close. Claire clenched her jaw as the program ran the password, thousands of numerals long just as she'd expected.

When Gage returned, Bray moved back and said, "We're in."

Gage came around the desk to watch as she copied the password into an e-mail message.

"E-mailing it to yourself?" Gage asked.

Claire hit Send. "Making sure that if we need to, we can get back in from anywhere."

Then she opened the protected sector of the Cranes-brook system that she'd never seen before. There were at least a dozen folders, probably hundreds of documents.

"Where to start?"

"That looks like it's going to take some time," Bray said. "I'll leave the two of you computer geeks to it and check out those labs to see what other memories I can scare up."

Though Claire didn't like Bray going off by himself, she couldn't stop him, so she didn't say anything. Maybe with him gone she could concentrate.

Gage pulled up a chair and parked himself next to her. "I've been trying to get into this baby for the last ten days."

"Welcome to the club."

Claire opened folder after folder to check the contents. Most files were filled with scientific data that had no meaning for her. But then she got to what looked like the original agreement between Cranesbrook Associates and DARPA—Defense Advanced Research Projects Agency—an arm of the Department of Defense.

"Here we go," she murmured, opening it.

She and Gage read the document simultaneously, and when they finished, they stared at each other in shocked silence.

"Unconscionable," Claire murmured.

Cranesbrook had been developing a bio-chemical weapon that would be delivered by missile. Its intent—to change brain function, turning its victims into virtual zombies.

BRAY STARTED IN the first of the three labs connected to Project Cypress. Two walls were filled with rat cages, and when he turned on the room lights, there was a lot of scurrying and squeaking.

"Hey, fellas," he murmured. "I'm not here to experiment on you, so relax. Just consider me a fellow lab rat."

Not that his assurances did any good. The scurrying and squeaking continued, but oddly enough, the activity seemed to be coming from the wall on the left. The rats in the cages on the right didn't make a sound. They didn't appear to be in great shape, either. They seemed subdued. Sick maybe. They looked at him through beady eyes that held no luster. Undoubtedly these rats had been forced to inhale the damn chemicals—poor guys—while the active rats were the control animals.

He touched one of the cages and felt a sense of panic. The room appeared distorted as did the men in the lab coats and the monkeys in cages along a third wall. Great, now he was picking up rat memories rather than the twisted human ones he was trying to find.

He let go and stared at the wall where the monkeys used to be kept. What the hell had happened to them? Had they been moved to a different lab?

Taking a tour of the room, Bray touched everything—tables, stools, equipment, empty vials. He saw chemicals being mixed. A caged rat being transported from the storeroom to a shelf. A monkey being given an injection and sinking into an unconscious heap. Unconscious? Or dead?

Spooked, Bray tried to pick up more about the monkey. Why would it have been killed?

About to leave, he decided to check the storeroom himself. He opened the door and a faint odor met him.

Bray froze. He'd smelled that same odor the night of the accident. The chemicals…

He closed his eyes and concentrated.

SUDDENLY he's on the floor, fighting his way up through a head that feels like it's split open, his stomach rumbling like he's going to puke up his guts.

"How the hell did it go wrong?"

He tries to focus on whoever is talking, but he can hardly open his eyes.

"I don't know, but the damage isn't that bad. No need to call the fire department."

He wants to tell them to call 9-1-1, but he can't find his voice.

"The experiment... The results are ruined!"

"Not necessarily. We'll get them over to Beech Grove Clinic as planned until we can see the results for ourselves."

As planned? He tries to lift his head, to see their faces to know who's speaking, but the room is whirling.

"And then what?"

"Dr. Morton will videotape them as instructed. And he'll make out a report as to how the chemicals affected these victims. And then when we don't need them any more..."

He doesn't finish, but the threat is clear.

BRAY JERKED BACK to the present. The memory had been his. He remembered that after hearing the threat, he'd backed himself out of the lab while the scientists had been busy with Gage and Vanderhoven. Somehow, he'd gotten the hell out of the building without them catching him. He'd puked up his guts as he'd stumbled toward the parking lot. And then a big blank. The next thing he remembered, he'd been at the marina. Panicked and looking for a place to hide.

A boat.

He pretty much knew the rest from there.

Now that he knew the truth, he really was a liability. The accident had been no accident. It had been planned to test the chemicals on human rats. Him and Gage. He didn't know if Vanderhoven had been part of it or if he'd simply been in the wrong place at the wrong time.

But one thing was certain—he and Gage had never been meant to live.

CLAIRE TOOK A BIG breath and said, "Our government really was ready to finance something this horrific?"

"It looks to me like this was simply meant to be a test, to see if it was possible."

Claire shook her head. "The monetary incentives were too great to be a what-if. Someone was pushing for this to happen."

After ascertaining the experiment was part of a Defense Science Office project called Controlling Neural Activity, she'd given over the computer to Gage, who seemed a lot calmer than she.

He said, "Colonel Ron Toren is the manager of the project. Toren has a reputation for going off half-cocked."

"And he's allowed to run rampant?"

"When fighting a really dangerous enemy, sometimes you have to think outside the box."

Gage's saying that sent a chill down her spine. "People who are exposed to these chemicals aren't going to be thinking much at all." While he seemed like a reasonable human being, years in the military— seeing all that combat, burying his friends—gave Gage a different perspective.

He was reading another document. "Here's the justification paper for investigating this solution." He glanced up at her. "Colonel Toren's contribution to the war on terrorism? Make the enemy docile, take away their aggression and they won't want to kill us anymore. Interesting. Then the military already in there could herd the enemy any way they wanted."

"But who is the enemy? Everyone? That chemical isn't going to distinguish between terrorists and women and their children."

"War doesn't distinguish—" Gage suddenly looked up as if he'd realized how upset she was becoming. "Sorry. I don't agree with any of this, but I was in combat too long to be surprised by anything."

"What they were trying to do and what actually happened… Something went wrong with the experiment. Bray needs to know about this. Maybe the information will kick-start some buried memory."

"Go tell him. I'll see what else I can find."

Sick inside, Claire went in search of Bray. Starting out cautiously, she hurried once she decided the corridors were clear. Then a low whistle made her practically jump out of her skin.

"Claire, over here!"

For a moment she thought she was seeing things, but no, that was her best friend standing at the end of the corridor, signaling to her. Her pulse began to speed through her veins and her throat grew tight. Her thoughts jumbled, she rushed toward Mac.

What was he doing here? How did he even get into the building without a security clearance?

Unless he *had* a security clearance…

"Oh, Mac, I'm so glad to see you." She didn't want to think about what his presence meant.

"Let's talk outside."

He inclined his head toward the door that led to the little nature preserve outside the lab wing. Though Claire had never seen anyone but an occasional gardener out there, she followed her friend who was already at the pond.

"Mac, talk to me. Tell me what the hell is going on."

"Sorry, Claire. You really need to get out of here now."

"Why? What will happen if I don't?"

"You'll end up like me."

"I don't understand."

Was he intimating he was part of the cover-up? Or had he been another failed human test?

"Just promise me you'll go and you won't look back. It's for your own good."

"Mac, please!"

Claire caught up to him and grabbed for his arm. Her hand cut right through air. She stared at him, at the handsome square-jawed, dark-eyed face she knew so well. The face she apparently didn't know at all.

"What the hell? What are you? Some kind of ghost?"

"Close, Claire. Close."

And then he faded to nothing.

Claire's heart pounded. What was going on? Was Mac alive or wasn't he? Was he able to project himself…

A projection!

The mastermind who'd projected a fake Gage to Echo had just done the same to her.

Had it been Mac himself?

She had to warn Bray!

Whirling around, she stopped herself before she went flying into the pond. The moon shone down on the water, and she could swear she saw something moving beneath the water's surface. Wanting to ignore it, wanting to go find Bray, she couldn't make her legs work. Couldn't take her eyes off the subtle waves in the water.

Her heart thundered in her chest as got down on one knee and plunged a hand into the water.

What the hell had she latched on to?

Solid…and yet not… Definitely unnatural…

She pulled out her hand and sat back, but the object drifted through the water up to her. Bloated fingers, flesh half-rotted off, class ring intact.

Her class! Rather, the male version of the one Mac had given to her.

The cry that escaped Claire echoed off the walls of the surrounding buildings. She'd finally gotten her wish, had finally found her best friend. He'd been right here, waiting for her to find him all along. Sobs broke from her and she turned away so she wouldn't be sick all over what was left of the one person who'd always been there for her.

It didn't seem right that her heart could break twice in the same night.

Chapter Eighteen

Thinking to surprise Echo by showing up unannounced, Rand was the one surprised when he saw the woman he loved leaving the house with Lily Darnell.

"Hey, what's going on? Where's Gage? Better yet, where are the two of you headed?"

"Gage and Bray are at Cranesbrook," Echo told him, her expression defiant. "They're going to prove their innocence."

"And you were planning to do what? Help them?"

"Yes," both women said in unison.

"What about Zoe?"

"The sitter's watching her."

Rand could see Echo had her back up. No doubt she assumed he was going to try to stop them. It took every ounce of strength not to act on that as instinct bade him. Echo was set on this. And Lily.

"I assume you two have a plan."

Lily said, "We were going to figure that out on the way there."

"Save me from impulsive women."

"You weren't saying that last night," Echo reminded

him. "And you promised me you would help clear my brother's name. It's time for you to stand up to your word, Rand. This is your chance."

Rand still wasn't sure Sloane was innocent even though Echo had told him about the security DVD being doctored. He'd already heard about Hank Riddell's murder and the fact that the locals caught Sloane red-handed. The last had seemed too convenient to him, though, especially since they'd been acting on an anonymous tip. He'd promised Echo he would try to clear her brother, and he feared that if he didn't come through with the goods this time, he would lose her forever.

"All right. I'll go, you stay."

"We're not waiting around, stewing until someone remembers to call us," Lily said.

Obviously the women were united in this. "Okay, how about you help me get into the place?"

Thinking he couldn't successfully play the cop card with security again, not on a Saturday night, Rand quickly explained his plan.

"Deal?" he ended.

Echo and Lily looked at each other and then at him. "Deal," they said in unison.

Then they all climbed into Echo's car and headed for Cranesbrook.

When they were just far enough away so they couldn't be seen by the security guard in the gatehouse, Rand got out of the car, and as agreed, punctured a tire. Air hissed out and he could see the car slowly settling down toward the pavement. He tapped the hood, slid back along the tree line and made his way toward the entrance.

Echo waited just long enough for him to get into position before putting the car in gear and rolling within spitting distance of the entrance gate. The car was tilted toward the collapsed tire, the difficulty obvious to anyone.

Echo stopped, and she and Lily both got out and walked over to check out the tire.

"It's flat, all right," Lily said, her words quavering. "Do you know how to change it?"

"Change a tire? Are you kidding?"

"What are we going to do now?"

Echo looked around as if panicked, then marched up to the guard house. The moment she engaged the guard's attention, Rand started moving closer.

"Excuse me, sir," Echo said, sounding pitiful, "but we need help. Flat tire."

"So call your service."

"I don't have a service."

"Then call a friend."

"No phone, and there's no one to call anyway. My brother isn't even available to help me tonight."

"We really have no one to save us but you," Lily said.

The guard didn't seem moved. He was being more difficult than Rand had imagined. He cursed silently as he waited for his opportunity to move in.

"I can call a tow truck for you," the guard offered.

Echo said, "I can't afford the fee. I just got that junker out of the shop and I'm broke."

"Same here," Lily said. "Can't you please help us? It'll only take a few minutes to change a tire, right?"

"Leave my station? I don't know."

"But we're right here in front of the entrance," Lily

insisted. "No one can get through that gate without you seeing."

"Please?" Echo begged, her voice sounding choked.

What a performance, Rand thought, getting ready to move as he saw her magic finally work on the security guard. He hadn't been sure Echo really could do helpless, but she was magnificent.

"All right," the guard said, leaving the gatehouse at last.

Rand waited until the man passed his hiding spot, then made his move. As Echo and Lily kept the guy's focus on them, he crossed the drive and slipped through the gatehouse and onto the grounds. The women hadn't liked being left out of the rest of the action, but they'd agreed it was more important for him to get inside Cranesbrook. Once the tire was changed, they would drive out of the guard's sight and wait for Rand's call.

He only hoped he wouldn't have cause to regret anything that happened tonight. The Feds were bound to be mightily displeased. This could bounce back on him professionally.

Worse, if he couldn't clear Brayden Sloane of any wrongdoing, he feared Echo would never be able to forgive him.

BRAY HAD GOTTEN what he could out of the new lab. The other night he'd gotten nothing from the old one. He decided to check out the storeroom in Lab 12 next.

Walking down the long corridor, he wondered what Claire and Gage had found. Whatever it was, it must be good to keep them both glued to the computer for so long.

He still couldn't believe Claire hadn't gotten out while the going was good. She must really love this Mac Ellroy. His throat constricted just thinking about it. About what she'd come to mean to him in such a short time. About what he didn't mean to her. He'd been nothing more than a damaged source of information.

Claire was stuck on a mystery man who apparently was alive and around, after all. And if Mac Ellroy proved to be part of the cover-up, Claire would be broken-hearted.

He was starting to think like a love-sick fool, Bray decided, shoving such thoughts into the back recesses of his mind as he entered Lab 12.

The area looked innocent enough. No evidence of a man having died there the day before. Had Riddell killed Artur or had he simply found the janitor après heart attack? Weird though, that the janitor had so conveniently died in a supposedly empty lab that was the hiding place for vials of chemicals.

Entering the storeroom, Bray searched the lower shelf behind the cleaning products. Whatever Claire had found there was gone now.

"Damn!"

He was about to get up when he spotted a small object on the floor. A cork like one that would top a test tube. Hesitating only a moment, he reached out and snatched it from the floor.

Touching the cork threw his brain into overdrive. He saw a man in a white lab coat pouring colored liquid from several vials into the metal bowl atop a black box. The next thing he knew, the scientist had set off the liquid and was breathing in the fumes.

His brain is on fire...
Bray grabbed his head.

HIS BRAIN is burning. Melting. And yet he's awake. He's inside, but the sun is blazing down on him. And the heat...the heat is becoming unbearable.

The sound of fire from an MP-5 whips him around, out of the storeroom and into the mountainous desert. What he sees there makes him nearly jump out of his skin.

"Why didn't you save me?" Taureen Morgan asks, his mouth a hole in a tight dark face that suddenly explodes into pink mist.

BRAY TRIED FIGHTING it, but he was losing. He was being thrown back to the Afghanistan conflict.

The enemy is everywhere...and this time he doesn't know if he can get out alive.

GRIEF GAVE WAY to cold fury. Claire wiped her eyes and got to her feet.

"I'll never forget you, Mac. And I won't let whoever killed you go free, I swear."

She said a quick prayer for his soul and then went to make good on her promise. When she arrived at the entrance to the corridor, the door was locked. That had been the bastard's motive, she assumed. Separate and conquer.

Running back to the pond, she picked up a rock and then approached one of the big lab windows. She hurled the rock as hard as she could. The tempered glass splintered, cracks spreading to encompass every inch. Then slowly the window bowed and began to cave in. The glass collapsed in balletic slow motion.

Claire removed her new suit jacket and used one of the sleeves to wipe down the bottom of the window frame and the ledge inside. Then she draped the jacket over the frame bottom and climbed into the lab.

She looked around for a weapon, but the best she could come up with was a fire extinguisher. Grabbing it off the wall, she left the lab only to stop dead when she came face to face with Dr. Martin Kelso.

Claire's heart began to thud. "Dr. Kelso…"

Would he try to make her see something that wasn't really there again?

His expression darkened. "Explain yourself, Ms. Fanshaw. Why are you here and what do you plan to do with that?" He gave the fire extinguisher in her hands an accusing glare.

"I'm here because of Project Cypress, Dr. Kelso, but I'm sure you already know that. As for the fire extinguisher…"

Before he could use his powers on her again, she launched the heavy metal missile at him. The fire extinguisher smacked him in the chest and head. He went down hard, crumpling to the floor like any ordinary man.

Strange noises shot along the corridor. From Lab 12? Bray! Claire ran.

When she opened the lab door, she froze. Instead of a lab with tables, she faced red rock and a desert floor. The sun blazed so hot, it immediately parched her. She looked around wildly. Backed into a far corner, Bray was in full military mode. Positioned in a crouch, his blank gaze roaming, he held an invisible weapon.

Kelso must have created the projection before getting back to her.

Claire started to move toward Bray, meaning to snap him out of his nightmare, when the skin at the back of her neck crawled. She slowly turned and faced the truth dressed in a white lab coat: Nelson Ulrich was the one wielding the new power.

Thinking fast, she used her own best weapon.

"I should have known you were the one, Dr. Ulrich." She said it with a hesitant smile, as though she were in awe of him. "You're so brilliant, it had to be you, of course."

He seemed taken aback for a moment, then asked, "Did you and Ellroy have a good reunion, Claire?"

Her stomach roiled at the reminder, but she kept her cool. This was the most difficult thing she'd ever done, but she moved smoothly toward him, an admiring smile still curving her lips as she asked, "How did you know about us?"

"His e-mail. Before I took care of Riddell, he finally got into Ellroy's e-mail for me. Imagine my surprise when I learned you were friends. How odd that you never said a thing about it."

"I'd wondered what happened to Mac, of course, but what I really wondered was how such a brilliant mind worked."

"I am brilliant," Ulrich agreed.

As she pulled the scientist's attention to her, the projection grew weaker. Claire glanced at Bray, who seemed confused when he looked down at his empty hands. His attention shifted to the scientist, and slowly he got to his feet.

He was coming out of it, Claire thought with relief.

"If I had known what you were doing from the beginning, Dr. Ulrich, I would have been at your side. Powerful men are like an aphrodisiac to me." She bit her lower lip and let a little moan escape her. "So talk dirty to me, tell me all about your creation."

The bastard grinned at her. He believed his own press!

"We were experimenting on controlling the neural pathways, taking away aggression," he told her. "That seemed to be working in our rats. But they refused to eat, started to die. The deadline was closing in, so when we modified the cocktail, we skipped the rats and went right to the monkeys. At first they were very sick, but they all came through it. And then I noticed a banana floating to one of the cages. The monkey was making it come to him. That's when I knew we had stumbled onto something far more valuable than we'd imagined."

"That must have been very satisfying for you." She bit her lip again and smiled at him.

He had to be thinking with something other than his brain, Claire realized, because the last of the projection dissipated. And judging from Bray's dark expression aimed at the scientist, he'd shaken off the projection's effects. Satisfied that this lie might have saved the life and mind of the man she loved, Claire backed away from Ulrich, who didn't seem to notice as he kept on boasting.

"I've never gotten the recognition I deserved. Not from the time I was a boy and threw myself into the one thing I was good at—science. My father punished me for being so weak. Now I'm the one doing the punishing."

Then Bray was on him, grabbing him by the front of his lab coat, lifting him as easily as if with telekinesis, when he was simply using his own brute strength.

"I intend to clear my name, Ulrich, and hand you over to the authorities."

Ulrich said, "You'll never have the chance, because you're going to die like the rest of them!"

Ulrich narrowed his eyes and Claire could feel the atmosphere in the room change. He was going to do it again. She tried not to panic.

"Bray, don't believe anything you see. Ulrich will plant lies in your mind. He's the one with the power of projection."

"Bitch!" Ulrich screeched at her, and the atmosphere stabilized.

As Bray threw Ulrich against a lab table in disgust, Claire heard a noise and turned to see Rand, gun drawn, standing in the doorway. Though the detective met her gaze, he didn't announce himself. He slipped back just outside the door.

"When did you get the bright idea of testing the chemicals on Gage and me?" Bray demanded.

"We had to have proof that the experiment would work on humans before we could offer it to the highest bidder."

"You were going to sell out your country? You would have been tried as a traitor."

"If caught," Ulrich corrected. "I didn't actually do the dirty work. I left that to Wes Vanderhoven. He understood the importance of the weapon we were creating. He volunteered to execute the test and got caught in the accident himself. When I saw how the chemicals worked on his and Darnell's brains, I experimented on myself."

"I remember hearing you tell Edmonston that you were sending us to Beech Grove Clinic where Dr. Morton was going to videotape us for you."

"Necessary proof of the success of the experiment."

"But you never meant for us to live."

Ulrich shrugged and a cruel smile twisted his mouth. "Alas, the chemicals killed you, after all."

"Like the monkeys?" Bray asked.

"We had to prevent the creatures from revealing our secrets. A necessary loss."

"Was Riddell a necessary loss, too?"

"It was only a matter of time before the little sycophant realized I had taken control of the situation. Besides, he'd served his purpose. He was no longer of any use to me."

Then Ulrich went silent and focused in on Bray, and suddenly the atmosphere changed fast. The lab immediately grew bright and hot. Claire looked around. The whole room was shifting, changing, again turning into something out of Bray's nightmare world.

Fearing Bray would succumb, that he wouldn't be able to fight the PTSD this time, she said, "Don't believe it, Bray. It's a lie. Ulrich is feeding you a lie. You're at Cranesbrook with me." She grabbed his hand. "Don't believe his lies. He'll try to kill you with them!"

Bray seemed to find strength in her grip as he said, "I know I'm at Cranesbrook with you, Claire."

Now some distance from them, Ulrich made a sound of disgust. He pulled two test tubes out of his lab coat pocket. "You won't be able to talk—neither of you— once you get a little whiff of this."

Ulrich launched the vials at them, but they stopped, suspended in midair as Gage entered the lab, followed closely by Rand.

"Oops," Claire said to Ulrich. "One of your experiments just went you one better."

"No!" Ulrich cried, reaching out and snatching the vials in his grip.

The two glass containers clinked together and the chemicals mixed, pouring over Ulrich's face. The scientist sucked some of the liquid in with a shriek. Gagging, he threw his hands to his head, and for a moment, Claire feared his head would explode. But in the end, his stomach merely emptied as he slid to the ground.

"Both of you, back away fast," Gage said, his expression intent on the fallen scientist. "The lunatic may have killed himself, but I don't want anyone else following."

Claire realized that Gage was using his power to keep the fumes from traveling toward them. Bray wrapped an arm around her back and pushed her to the doorway. Rand was already in the hall on his cell phone.

"Detective Rand McClellan. We have a bio-chem hazard at Cranesbrook Associates and need a HAZMAT team immediately."

Gage followed and closed the door behind them. "Let's go get some fresh air."

THE BASTARD hadn't died. Claire could hardly believe Dr. Nelson Ulrich was still alive, though in a way, his punishment was even worse. He'd lost his mind. Literally. He would be a vegetable for however long his body continued on. Without a directive indicating otherwise, that could be a long, long time.

Maybe in this case, the punishment fit the crime.

Thankfully, Dr. Kelso was okay. The only aftereffects of her knocking him out with the fire extinguisher were a sore shoulder and a mild headache. When he'd seen her so unexpectedly the night before, he'd actually thought she'd been involved in the underhanded dealings at Cranesbrook. As it was, he expected her to turn in her resignation, but he wasn't going to press charges.

"We need to decide what we're going to do," Bray told the others. "We all have a stake in this, so everyone needs to agree."

A night of debriefing during which they'd carefully avoided straight talk about Bray's and Gage's powers had followed a mutual decision to outright lie, a decision they'd made before the authorities had shown up. They'd created a story woven out of half-truths. Claire had thought it amazingly convincing, and she hadn't even contributed to the lie. She'd merely repeated it.

Halfway through the morning, they'd been released and had all convened at Bray's home for a late breakfast and now for a serious conversation.

"We can't let anyone know about the powers," Lily said. "Ever. Or Gage and Bray will be a freak show. They'll cage them like animals and say it's for their own protection."

"If we don't ever use them, no one will know," Bray said.

"Right," Gage agreed. "Telekinesis—what's that?"

"They're going to learn about what happened from the research notes," Echo predicted. "It's only a matter of time."

Claire didn't say anything. Echo was correct, of course. Somehow, though, she didn't feel as if she had a right to express her opinion, so she stayed on the fringe of the group and kept her mouth shut. She'd forced herself into the situation, while they'd all simply been victims. She would do anything they required of her.

Her eyes stung with unshed tears as she thought again about Mac, who'd been taken away in a body bag. There would be an autopsy, but at least, when the medical examiner was through with him, she could see that he had a proper burial.

"Thinking about using Ulrich's research in reality is the scariest thing I can think of," Gage said. "What would happen if the wrong people got their hands on it?"

"What if the 'right' people took it to the ultimate level?" Rand said. "No one should have these kinds of powers. No offense intended," he said directly to Bray.

"None taken."

"We don't have any control about what happens." Echo shook her head. "I mean, we can't say anything, but once informed scientists get to those research notes… There's just nothing we can do to stop this train from leaving the station."

Knowing what she had to do, Claire finally spoke up. "Actually, there is."

Everyone turned to her. She connected with Bray who'd been unlike himself since they'd left the lab. He'd been distant and seeming in some dark place. He hadn't spoken to her directly once until now.

"Tell us," he said.

"It depends on whether or not you're comfortable living another lie for the rest of your lives." She was speaking to them all, but looking straight into his eyes. "If everyone doesn't agree to this and keep the pact, it'll come down on Bray and Gage and on me like a ton of bricks."

"None of us is going to talk about what really happened," Lily said. "But how does that negate the research notes?"

"What if every Project Cypress file was destroyed?"

"You can do that?" Gage asked. "Infect them with a virus that can't be doctored?"

"I can find a way."

"Why not just delete them?" Lily asked.

"Because they'd still be like ghosts on the hard drives at Cranesbrook," Rand told her, no doubt following Claire's way of thinking. "Someone could bring them back unless they're overwritten. What about other notes? What if Ulrich kept a journal?"

"We just have to hope he didn't, or if he did, we have to hope that the authorities put whatever he says to the ravings of a madman," Claire said. "It's more likely he kept the information where he thought no one could get their hands on it, though."

"Then I say destroy the damn files and we all stand behind you," Rand said.

A chorus of voices lent their agreement, including Bray's, so Claire fetched her laptop and settled herself in his office to work. At some point, she realized Bray came in and sat behind her and watched her work.

He didn't say a word.

Neither did she.

Once online, she tapped into a network of Black-hats—computer hackers who could and would do anything for pay or even for their own amusement.

Quickly letting them in on her "theoretical" problem, she was offered a series of solutions, the best of which was layering—first replacing the data, then having a virus corrupt the fake data and having a virus bomb ready to corrupt it yet again when someone tried to get in. A triple play.

It took her several hours, but when she was done, she was as confident as she could be that no one was going to get anything of value from the Project Cypress files.

Spinning in her chair, she said, "Done."

"You do this often?"

"Never before."

"Can I believe that?"

Claire sighed. "It's up to you to decide what you believe and what you don't, Bray. Maybe I've told too many lies for you to trust me, but I never told a lie that was meant to hurt anyone."

"Then why do it at all? You're really, really good at it."

"I learned from the best. A mother who hid her alcoholism and expected her kids to do the same for her when the social worker came around. Considering the depths of my so-called family, I lied just to protect myself. I did get really good at creating a fantasy life to fool my friends and my teachers, and maybe I didn't know when to stop. I don't expect you to understand. But I hope you believe that I didn't mean to break anyone's heart," she said, meaning his, of course.

"I understand that you needed to find out what happened to Ellroy."

"He was my best friend, Bray. He was the only one I could count on for most of my life. We might not have been related by blood, but he was my family, just like the people in the other room are yours." She couldn't bring herself to count on them accepting her. Probably she would never see them again once Project Cypress became a thing of the past. "I couldn't just let Mac go like he didn't mean anything. Like the way my mom and my siblings did to me."

"I get it," Bray said, his expression opening. "I'm really sorry he didn't make it and that you had to find him the way you did. I don't expect you to ever let go of him. Or the memory of him. But maybe it's time you let go of the lies."

Claire couldn't help the tears that filled her eyes as she thought about the future. Mac was gone and now she was left with no one. The future stretched out in front of her empty and grim.

Then Bray took her in his arms and held her tight against him. "Cry if you want."

"I don't want to cry anymore. I want to be happy." Suddenly, Claire wanted to tell him the truth she'd been holding back since he'd insulted her the night before. But would he believe her? "I want to love you, Bray."

"Then love me."

"I already do, with my whole heart. The question is…will you let me? And do you believe me?"

"Maybe the chemicals addled my brain, because I do believe you. I lied to you when I said you were nothing to me. I was trying to protect you."

"I know."

"That and the other things that happened last night gave me a lot to think about," he admitted. "How your lies got to Ulrich and saved me…the fact that we all lied to the authorities to keep this abomination from spreading. I guess making the decision of what to tell other people isn't always black or white."

Her chest was tight with hope when she looked up at him. "Can we start over?"

"Why don't we pick up where we left off?" he murmured just before he kissed her.

Epilogue

Two months after the accident

"Ho-ho-ho." Dressed in a Santa suit, Bray picked up a gaily wrapped present from under the fresh spruce whose top touched the ceiling and whose boughs were loaded with lights and ornaments Echo had collected over the years. "Have you been a good little girl?" He set the present on the floor in front of Zoe and grinned behind his white beard as his niece squealed and began ripping off the paper.

"Hey, Santa, what do you have for me tonight?" Claire asked softly.

"Whatever your heart desires."

Her smile lit up her face and Bray thought that dressed in her green outfit, she made the most beautiful elf in the world.

They were all gathered in Echo's home for eggnog, cookies and Christmas carols, all part of an old-fashioned Christmas Eve—Rand, of course, who couldn't keep his eyes off Echo; Gage and Lily, who couldn't keep their hands off each other; and Claire, who couldn't stop smiling at him.

Bray still couldn't believe he was lucky enough to have her love him as much as he did her.

"I have one other gift here," he said in his Santa voice. From his bag, he pulled out a smallish present, the one he'd been told to leave for last. "Echo, have you been a good girl this year?"

"Have I?" she asked Rand.

"Sometimes you've been good, but other times you've been really, really sensational."

They gave each other such a loopy grin that Bray had to insert himself to deliver the present. "For you."

Echo took it and ripped off the paper with every bit of abandon as had her daughter. She stared at the small jeweler's box in her hand for a moment before opening it. Her mouth rounded into an O.

"Merry Christmas, Echo," Rand said. "Can I help you put that on?"

"That" being a substantial diamond ring, Bray noted.

"Uh-huh," she said, handing him the box and holding out both hands, fingers spread. "You pick the finger."

Slipping it on her left ring finger, he said, "Marry me and make me the happiest man in the world."

Echo squealed, threw her arms around his neck and covered his face with kisses. "Yes…yes…yes!"

"Time to break out the bubbly," Claire said. She popped open a bottle.

"As soon as my condo sells," Rand told Bray, "I want to pay you back what you put into this house."

"Not necessary. I did it for my sister."

"But we're going to be family, and I'm going to take care of Echo and Zoe now."

Bray shook Rand's hand. "And you'd better do a damn fine job of it or you'll answer to me."

Claire passed around a tray with filled champagne glasses. Lifting her own glass, she said, "To love that lasts a lifetime."

They all drank. All but Lily.

Gage frowned down on his wife. "Something wrong with your champagne?"

Lily sighed. "I have a present for you that Santa simply *can't* deliver. We're going to have a baby."

"Looks like I should've hung around home sooner."

Gage threw his arms around his wife, and Bray thought he'd never seen his ex-partner appear so happy.

So that Gage could pursue developing his inventions, he'd sold his half of Five Star Security to Claire. Bray's new partner said she'd finally found something to compete with her love of computers. Bray wasn't sure if she meant the business or him, but he decided to take it very personally.

The security business was thriving after the publicity they'd gotten in taking down Nelson Ulrich, a mad scientist who'd run amuck as far as anyone knew. No one had ever found out the real secrets of Project Cypress. Ulrich had been kept alive by machines for several weeks before he'd passed on, his secrets buried with him, as far as they were all concerned.

No matter how happy everyone else in the room might be, Bray thought he was the happiest. He'd been seeing a therapist and had been making great strides in dealing with the PTSD. Most of all, he had Claire by his side, both in work and in life. Nothing like a reformed woman to keep him challenged during the day and warm at night.

When she said, "Hey, Santa, about that special Christmas present—that would be you," he knew she was being truthful.

"You already have me for as long as you want me."

She indicated the mistletoe hanging over their heads. He didn't miss a beat. He kissed her, beard and all.

"Let's get out of here," Claire whispered, pulling him toward the door. "Santa needs to give me that present in private."

"Merry Christmas to all," Bray boomed to the others. "And to all a good night."

* * * * *

Experience entertaining women's fiction
for every woman who has wondered "what's next?"
in their lives.
Turn the page for a sneak preview of a new book
from Harlequin NEXT
WHY IS MURDER ON THE MENU, ANYWAY?
by Stevi Mittman

On Sale December 26, wherever books are sold.

"Now that's the kind of man you should be looking for,"
my mother, the self-appointed keeper of my shelf-life
stamp, says. She points with her fork at a man in the
corner of The Steak-Out Restaurant, a dive I've just
been hired to redecorate. Making this restaurant look
four-star will be hard, but not half as hard as getting
through lunch without strangling the woman across the
table from me. "*He* would make a good husband."

"Oh, you can tell that from across the room?" I ask,
wondering how it is she can forget that when we had
trouble getting rid of my last husband, she shot him.
"Besides being ten minutes away from death if he

actually eats all that steak, he's twenty years too old for me and—shallow woman that I am—twenty pounds too heavy. Besides, I am *so* not looking for another husband here. I'm looking to design a new image for this place, looking for some sense of ambience, some feeling, something I can build a proposal on for them."

My mother studies the man in the corner, tilting her head, the better to gauge his age, I suppose. I think she's grimacing, but with all the Botox and Restylane injected into that face, it's hard to tell. She takes another bite of her steak salad, chews slowly so that I don't miss the fact that the steak is a poor cut and tougher than it should be. "You're concentrating on the wrong kind of proposal," she says finally. "Just look at this place, Teddi. It's a dive. There are hardly any other diners. What does *that* tell you about the food?"

"That they cater to a dinner crowd and it's lunchtime," I tell her.

I don't know what I was thinking bringing her here with me. I suppose I thought it would be better than eating alone. There really are days when my common sense goes on vacation. Clearly, this is one of them. I mean really, did I not resolve less than three weeks ago that I would not let my mother get to me anymore?

What good are New Year's resolutions, anyway?

Mario approaches the man's table and my mother studies him while they converse. Eventually Mario leaves the table with a huff, after which the diner glances up and meets my mother's gaze. I think she's smiling at him. That or she's got indigestion. They size each other up.

I concentrate on making sketches in my notebook and try to ignore the fact that my mother is flirting. At nearly seventy, she's developed an unhealthy interest in members of the opposite sex to whom she isn't married.

According to my father, who has broken the TMI rule and given me Too Much Information, she has no interest in sex with him. Better, I suppose, to be clued in on what they aren't doing in the bedroom than have to hear what they might be.

"He's not so old," my mother says, noticing that I have barely touched the Chinese chicken salad she warned me not to get. "He's got about as many years on you as you have on your little cop friend."

She does this to make me crazy. I know it, but it works all the same. "Drew Scoones is not my little 'friend.' He's a detective with whom I—"

"Screwed around," my mother says. I must look shocked, because my mother laughs at me and asks if I think she doesn't know the "lingo."

What I thought she didn't know was that Drew and I actually tangled the sheets. And, since it's possible she's just fishing, I sidestep the issue and tell her that Drew is just a couple of years younger than me and that I don't need reminding. I dig into my salad with renewed vigor, determined to show my mother that Chinese chicken salad in a steak place was not the stupid choice it's proving to be.

After a few more minutes of my picking at the wilted leaves on my plate, the man my mother has me nearly engaged to pays his bill and heads past us toward the back of the restaurant. I watch my mother take in his shoes, his suit and the diamond pinkie ring that seems to be cutting off the circulation in his little finger.

"Such nice hands," she says after the man is out of sight. "Manicured." She and I both stare at my hands. I have two popped acrylics that are being held on at weird angles by bandages. My cuticles are ragged and there's marker decorating my right hand from measuring carelessly when I did a drawing for a customer.

Twenty minutes later she's disappointed that he managed to leave the restaurant without our noticing. He will join the list of the ones I let get away. I will hear about him twenty years from now when—according to my mother—my children will be grown and I will still be single, living pathetically alone with several dogs and cats.

After my ex, that sounds good to me.

The waitress tells us that our meal has been taken care of by the management and, after thanking Mario, the owner, complimenting him on the wonderful meal and assuring him that once I have redecorated his place people will be flocking here in droves (I actually use those words and ignore my mother when she rolls her eyes), my mother and I head for the restroom.

My father—unfortunately not with us today—has the patience of a saint. He got it over the years of living with my mother. She, perhaps as a result, figures he has the patience for both of them, and feels justified having none. For her, no rules apply, and a little thing like a picture of a man on the door to a public restroom is certainly no barrier to using the john. In all fairness, it does seem silly to stand and wait for the ladies' room if no one is using the men's room.

Still, it's the idea that rules don't apply to her, signs don't apply to her, conventions don't apply to her. She knocks on the door to the men's room. When no one answers she gestures to me to go ahead in. I tell her that I can certainly wait for the ladies' room to be free and she shrugs and goes in herself.

Not a minute later there is a blood-curdling scream from behind the men's room door.

"Mom!" I yell. "Are you all right?"

Mario comes running over, the waitress on his heels. Two customers head our way while my mother continues to scream.

I try the door, but it is locked. I yell for her to open it and she fumbles with the knob. When she finally manages to unlock and open it, she is white behind her two streaks of blush, but she is on her feet and appears shaken but not stirred.

"What happened?" I ask her. So do Mario and the waitress and the few customers who have migrated to the back of the place.

She points toward the bathroom and I go in, thinking it serves her right for using the men's room. But I see nothing amiss.

She gestures toward the stall, and, like any self-respecting and suspicious woman, I poke the door open with one finger, expecting the worst.

What I find is worse than the worst.

The husband my mother picked out for me is sitting on the toilet. His pants are puddled down around his ankles, his hands are hanging at his sides. Pinned to his chest is some sort of Health Department certificate.

Oh, and there is a large, round, bloodless bullet hole between his eyes.

* * *

Four Nassau County police officers are securing the area, waiting for the detectives and crime scene personnel to show up. They are trying, though not very hard, to comfort my mother, who in another era would be considered to be suffering from the vapors. Less tactful in the twenty-first century, I'd say she was losing it. That is, if I didn't know her better, know she was milking it for everything it was worth.

My mother loves attention. As it begins to flag, she swoons and claims to feel faint. Despite four No Smoking signs, my mother insists it's all right for her to light up because, after all, she's in shock. Not to mention that signs, as we know, don't apply to her.

When asked not to smoke, she collapses mournfully in a chair and lets her head loll to the side, all without mussing her hair.

Eventually, the detectives show up to find the four patrolmen all circled around her, debating whether to administer CPR, smelling salts or simply call the paramedics. I, however, know just what will snap her to attention.

"Detective Scoones," I say loudly. My mother parts the sea of cops.

"We have to stop meeting like this," he says lightly to me, but I can feel him checking me over with his eyes, making sure I'm all right while pretending not to care.

"What have you got in those pants?" my mother asks him, coming to her feet and staring at his crotch accusingly. "*Baydar*? Everywhere we Bayers are, you turn up. You don't expect me to buy that this is a coincidence, I hope."

Drew tells my mother that it's nice to see her, too, and asks if it's his fault that her daughter seems to attract disasters.

Charming to be made to feel like the bearer of a plague.

He asks how I am.

"Just peachy," I tell him. "I seem to be making a habit of finding dead bodies, my mother is driving me crazy and the catering hall I book two freakin' years ago for Dana's bat mitzvah has just been shut down by the Board of Health!"

"Glad to see your luck's finally changing," he says, giving me a quick squeeze around the shoulders before turning his attention to the patrolmen, asking what they've got, whether they've taken any statements, moved anything, all the sort of stuff you see on TV, without any of the drama. That is, if you don't count my mother's threats to faint every few minutes when she senses no one paying attention to her.

Mario tells his wait staff to bring everyone espresso, which I decline because I'm wired enough. Drew pulls him aside and a minute later I'm handed a cup of coffee that smells divinely of Kahlúa.

The man knows me well. Too well.

His partner, whom I've met once or twice, says he'll interview the kitchen staff. Drew asks Mario if he minds if he takes statements from the patrons first and gets to him and the wait staff afterward.

"No, no," Mario tells him. "Do the patrons first." Drew raises his eyebrow at me like he wants to know if I get the double entendre. I try to look bored.

"What it is with you and murder victims?" he asks me when we sit down at a table in the corner.

I search them out so that I can see you again, I almost say, but I'm afraid it will sound desperate instead of sarcastic.

My mother, lighting up and daring him with a look to tell her not to, reminds him that *she* was the one to find the body.

Drew asks what happened *this time*. My mother tells him how the man in the john was "taken" with me, couldn't take his eyes off me and blatantly flirted with both of us. To his credit, Drew doesn't laugh, but his smirk is undeniable to the trained eye. And I've had my eye trained on him for nearly a year now.

"While he was noticing you," he asks me, "did *you* notice anything about him? Was he waiting for anyone? Watching for anything?"

I tell him that he didn't appear to be waiting or watching. That he made no phone calls, was fairly intent on eating and did, indeed, flirt with my mother. This last bit Drew takes with a grain of salt, which was the way it was intended.

"And he had a short conversation with Mario," I tell him. "I think he might have been unhappy with the food, though he didn't send it back."

Drew asks what makes me think he was dissatisfied, and I tell him that the discussion seemed acrimonious and that Mario looked distressed when he left the table. Drew makes a note and says he'll look into it and asks about anyone else in the restaurant. Did I see anyone who didn't seem to belong, anyone who was watching the victim, anyone looking suspicious?

"Besides my mother?" I ask him, and Mom huffs and blows her cigarette smoke in my direction.

I tell him that there were several deliveries, the kitchen staff going in and out the back door to grab a smoke. He stops me and asks what I was doing checking out the back door of the restaurant.

Proudly—because, while he was off forgetting me, dropping by only once in a while to say hi to Jesse, my son, or drop something by for one of my daughters that he thought they might like, I was getting on with my life—I tell him that I'm decorating the place.

He looks genuinely impressed. "Commercial customers? That's great," he says. Okay, that's what he *ought* to say. What he actually says is, "Whatever pays the bills."

"Howard Rosen, the famous restaurant critic, got her the job," my mother says. "You met him—the good-looking, distinguished gentleman with the *real* job, something to be proud of. I guess you've never read his reviews in *Newsday*."

Drew, without missing a beat, tells her that Howard's reviews are on the top of his list, as soon as he learns how to read.

"I only meant—" my mother starts, but both of us assure her that we know just what she meant.

"So," Drew says. "Deliveries?"

I tell him that Mario would know better than I, but that I saw vegetable come in, maybe fish and linens.

"This is the second restaurant job Howard's got her," my mother tells Drew.

"At least she's getting *something* out of the relationship," he says.

"If he were here," my mother says, ignoring the insinuation, "he'd be comforting her instead of interrogating her. He'd be making sure we're both all right after such an ordeal."

"I'm sure he would," Drew agrees, then looks me in the eyes as if he's measuring my tolerance for shock. Quietly he adds, "But then maybe he doesn't know just what strong stuff your daughter's made of."

It's the closest thing to a tender moment I can expect from Drew Scoones. My mother breaks the spell. "She gets that from me," she says.

Both Drew and I take a minute, probably to pray that's all I inherited from her.

"I'm just trying to save you some time and effort," my mother tells him. "My money's on Howard."

Drew withers her with a look and mutters something that sounds suspiciously like "Fool's gold." Then he excuses himself to go back to work.

I catch his sleeve and ask if it's all right for us to leave. He says sure, he knows where we live. I say goodbye to Mario. I assure him that I will have some sketches for him in a few days, all the while hoping that this murder doesn't cancel his redecorating plans. I need the money desperately, the alternative being borrowing from my parents and being strangled by the strings.

My mother is strangely quiet all the way to her house. She doesn't tell me what a loser Drew Scoones is—despite his good looks—and how I was obviously drooling over him. She doesn't ask me where Howard is taking me tonight or warn me not to tell my father about what happened because he will worry about us both and no doubt insist we see our respective psychiatrists.

She fidgets nervously, opening and closing her purse over and over again.

"You okay?" I ask her. After all, she's just found a dead man on the toilet, and tough as she is that's got to be upsetting.

When she doesn't answer me I pull over to the side of the road.

"Mom?" She refuses to meet my eyes. "You want me to take you to see Dr. Cohen?"

She looks out the window as if she's just realized we're on Broadway in Woodmere. "Aren't we near Marvin's Jewelers?" she asks, pulling something out of her purse.

"What have you got, Mother?" I ask, prying open her fingers to find the murdered man's ring.

"It was on the sink," she says in answer to my dropped jaw. "I was going to get his name and address and have you return it to him so that he could ask you out. I thought it was a sign that the two of you were meant to be together."

"He's dead, Mom. You understand that, right?" I ask. You never can tell when my mother is fine and when she's in la-la land.

"Well, I didn't know that," she shouts at me. "Not at the time."

I ask why she didn't give it to Drew, realize that she wouldn't give Drew the time in a clock shop and add, "...or one of the other policemen?"

"For heaven's sake," she tells me. "The man is dead, Teddi, and I took his ring. How would that look?"

Before I can tell her it looks just the way it is, she pulls out a cigarette and threatens to light it.

"I mean really," she says, shaking her head like it's my brains that are loose. "What does he need with it now?"

nocturne™

WAS HE HER SAVIOR
OR HER NIGHTMARE?

HAUNTED
LISA CHILDS

Years ago, Ariel and her sisters were separated for
their own protection. Now the man who vowed
revenge on her family has resumed the hunt, and
Ariel must warn her sisters before it's too late.
The closer she comes to finding them, the more
secretive her fiancé becomes. Can she trust the man
she plans to spend eternity with? Or has he been
waiting for the perfect moment to destroy her?

On sale December 2006.

SNHDEC

In February, expect MORE
from

HARLEQUIN® Romance®

as it increases to six titles per month.

What's to come...

Rancher and Protector

Part of the

Western Weddings
miniseries

BY JUDY CHRISTENBERRY

The Boss's Pregnancy Proposal

BY RAYE MORGAN

Don't miss February's
incredible line up of authors!

REQUEST YOUR FREE BOOKS!

2 FREE NOVELS PLUS 2 FREE GIFTS!

HARLEQUIN®
INTRIGUE®

Breathtaking Romantic Suspense

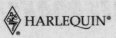

 HARLEQUIN®

INTRIGUE®

COMING NEXT MONTH

#963 OPERATION: MIDNIGHT COWBOY by Linda Castillo
When agent-turned-cowboy Bo Ruskin is tasked to shelter
Rachael Armitage at his remote Wyoming ranch, nothing stays
hidden—not even this cowboy's damaging secret—as they're hunted
by a brutal crime lord.

#964 UNDER THE MICROSCOPE by Jessica Andersen
Investigator Maximilian Vasek suffers from damsel in distress syndrome.
So when his favorite damsel, Raine Montgomery, is targeted while
developing a medical breakthrough, he's going to have a hard time
breaking bad habits—and not hearts.

#965 SIX-GUN INVESTIGATION by Mallory Kane
The Silver Star of Texas
In the town of Justice, investigative reporter Anna Wallace is playing
havoc with Renaissance cowboy Zane McKinney's organized murder
investigation. But was what happened in the Justice Hotel all that odd
for a town with a history of violence?

#966 BEAST IN THE TOWER by Julie Miller
He's a Mystery
Dr. Damon Sinclair lives in his penthouse lab above Kansas City.
Thirty floors below, Kit Snow finds herself inexplicably drawn to this
shadowy man.

#967 THE BODYGUARD CONTRACT by Donna Young
Lara Mercer's latest mission: retrieve a lethal biochemical agent before
it's released into Las Vegas. But her backup is ex-lover Ian MacAlister, a
government operative taught that love and duty don't mix.

**#968 THE AMERICAN TEMP AND THE BRITISH
INSPECTOR by Pat White**
The Blackwell Group
When Max Templeton is assigned to lead the Blackwell Group, he
brings along his girl Friday Cassie Clarke to find the Crimson Killer—
Max's only unfinished case.